can't help but want you

TAY MO'NAE

one

Brenna Tucker

The wedding…

"COME DANCE WITH ME." Tae held his hand out for me to grasp.

Frowning, I stared at it before slowly dragging my eyes back to his. "*I don't even like you.*"

Aisha and Gage laughed, but I was serious. Trying to get Tae out of my system wasn't an easy task, but it was something I was determined to do. The two of us connected in a way I never had with anyone else. It could have been because I had known him for years.

Being best friends with his little sister meant being in Tae's presence a lot throughout the years. I always found myself sneaking glances at him. Even though I never acted on anything, I couldn't miss how attractive he had always been.

Devontae King was six feet, bowlegged, and bulked up over the years due to his strict workout regimen. He kept his hair short in Caesar cut. His face always sported a well lined up mustache that hooded his thick, skin tone lips and a five o'clock shadow that gave him a little rugged look.

Right now, staring up at him had my stomach fluttering like crazy. His golden brown skin glowed under the illuminated lights in the reception hall.

"Yeah, don't do me like that. We used to have a lot of fun together." The double entendre in his words caused a shock to shoot down to my lower lips and my breathing to stagger. I tried not to think about how his large, rough hands used to work my body over. Tae had learned my spots with ease and having sex with him was always on another level. Maybe it was because of the years I'd known him, but sex with him always felt different from other men I had been with.

Heat filled my center.

Clearing my throat, I pushed those thoughts away. Now wasn't the time to reminisce. I was moving on, and we were currently at my best friend's wedding. My eyes shifted over to her and Gage. The two had been through a lot, yet here they were two kids later tying the knot. I was happy for both of them. There weren't two people that deserved each other more than them.

Pushing out a deep breath, I stared back at Tae, who was still standing there with his hand out.

"Just one dance." Playfully I rolled my eyes and grabbed his hand.

The fluttering in my stomach intensified when we got to the dance floor. My hands went to his shoulders and his to my waist. Instantly he pulled me closer. My nipples pebbled at the contact.

I closed my eyes attempting to ignore the raging sensations shooting through my body. This was the first time I had been this close to Tae in months. Once I found out he had a baby on the way, I ended whatever it was we had going on. I had nothing against kids, especially those I could give back to their parents, but being a mom wasn't on my agenda. It pained me to step away from Tae, but I knew it was something I had to do.

"I forgot how good you felt in my arms." Tae's warm breath kissed my ear, causing the hairs on my neck to rise. A shiver shot down my spine.

I inhaled a sharp breath, choosing not to answer. A low chuckle fell from his lips as his grip tightened around me. I could feel his dick press against my stomach.

I wasn't even listening to the song that was playing, but somehow our bodies moved in sync with the beat. Closely we swayed together in silence. For a moment, it felt like the issues between us didn't exist. The two of us always argued as if we hated each other, but when it was just me and Tae that was never the case. The two of us were never exclusive, and I was aware he did whatever in his spare time, but when the two of us were together none of that mattered. I always enjoyed being around him regardless of how we acted around other people.

"You don't miss me, B?" Tae broke the silence between us. He pulled back and stared me in the face. For a moment, I got lost in his Cognac hooded eyes.

"Does that really matter?" My head tilted to the side, and a small toothless smile formed on my face.

One corner of his mouth lifted. "To me, it does." My thumb brushed across the tattoo of scattered doves on his neck.

His voice dropped and his eyes grew a shade darker.

I went to step back, but he held me tighter. "Where you going, B? We can't have a conversation now?"

I rolled my eyes. "You asked for a dance, not a therapy session."

Again, a low chuckle fell from his mouth. "A'right, I see you on your bullshit today." His head bobbed. My smile grew.

"Shut up!" I giggled.

My head leaned forward and I rested my forehead on his wide chest. A sense of comfort filled me.

"I do miss you, Tae," I spoke lowly after a few minutes. "I've known you most of my life, and when things took an unexpected turn between us, I enjoyed it. I had fun with you while it lasted."

My words were low, but I knew he heard me by how his body reacted as I spoke. Closing my eyes, I took in his rich scent.

His heartbeat brought harmony to me. It was easy to get lost in Tae. He was one of the most down to earth people I'd ever met. He was open with his emotions and what he wanted. One thing I always loved was even though I was more closed off, he was always able to get me to open up.

"Uncle Tae!" Bailey came rushing up to us and tugged on Tae's suit jacket. "You said we would dance!" She pouted.

Pulling away from Tae, I exhaled deeply before smiling down at my Goddaughter.

"Oh yeah, I did, didn't I!" Tae bent down and scooped his niece up, causing her to squeal in giggles. The love he had for Bailey before and after Gage came into the picture was beautiful. He always made sure she never lacked a male figure and loved her like she was his. For a second, I pictured him with his son. Although becoming a father was unexpected news, I know he was an amazing father. Tae was a naturally nurturing man.

"I'll leave y'all to it." I reached up and brushed my hand over Bailey's head.

Tae looked at me with questioning eyes. I knew there was more he wanted to talk about. That was Tae; he didn't like to leave shit in the air. He was big on communication and resolving issues. On the other hand, I'd rather just let shit ride.

Making my way to the open bar, I ordered a *Blue Muthafucka* and leaned against the bar while the bartender made my drink.

My eyes swept across the hall and my heart swelled. It wasn't easy putting this wedding together. There was a lot of pressure on me to ensure everything came together without any issues. Knowing that Aisha's and Gage's wedding would be televised made my job ten times more stressful. I made sure never to show my worries to Aisha because she had enough going on at the time, but I was scared shitless.

Her wedding was the biggest event I had ever planned since taking the leap of faith and starting my own business. *Picture This Event and Planning* was my baby, and I took it seriously. I knew if Aisha's wedding went well, it could open many more doors for me.

"Here you are," the bartender spoke from behind me.

Turning slightly, I thanked him and grabbed my drink.

Going back to observing the room while sipping my drink, an overwhelming feeling warmed my chest. There were a lot of people here, most I didn't know. Gage was a big deal, especially since his rebrand and amazing last season. Although the cameras were gone, the celebrities and influencers were still present.

Locking my eyes on the Kings, I dropped my attention down to the car seat sitting next to Tae's mom. I couldn't see the baby, but I assumed he was sleeping. Candace was speaking to her husband and Gage's parents while rocking the car seat back and forth softly.

Tae's son was adorable, and even though I had only seen him once, I knew he favored his daddy. I hadn't met his child's mother personally, but from what I was told, she was a piece of work.

Snatching my eyes from them, I found the newly married couple. Aisha was sitting on her husband's lap, being fed cake, while his hands rested on her bulging belly. She smiled brightly, happily eating from his hands, and he stared at her with gleaming eyes.

Taking a big swig of my drink, I made my way back to their table where my purse was.

"Look at y'all looking all happy and in love!" I gushed, taking a seat and grabbing my purse. Sitting down, I pulled my phone out and it lit up with notifications.

A message from Randy, the guy I was currently seeing, popped up on the screen.

"You and my brother looked cozy," Aisha mentioned gaining my attention for a moment.

"I mean, we're still friends." With a slight shrug of the shoulders, I focused back on my phone.

Randy: *I hate I wasn't able to come with you.*

Things with Randy were still new. I wasn't sure if things would go deeper than they were, but I was enjoying his company. Things were fun for now, and we were exploring the thought of getting serious. Still, bringing him around my close friends wasn't something I was ready for. It didn't matter though because Randy had a prior engagement tonight anyway.

"Why you just won't make things right with my boy? It's not like y'all gotta be a secret anymore," Gage commented, grinning.

"I'm confused about what I'm supposed to make right. Tae and I were having fun, that's it."

"Damn, tell me how you really feel." My eyes shot up to Tae approaching our table with his son in his arms. The sight was bittersweet for me. Seeing an active father with his kid was a beautiful thing, but at the same time, I knew it was why Tae and I couldn't be together.

"Oooo, let me see my baby!" Aisha gushed, hurrying off Gage's lap as fast as her stomach allowed. She snatched her nephew from her brother's arms and smothered him in kisses.

"Come with me really quick." Tae's eyes were locked on me.

They appeared darker than normal. For some reason, my stomach flipped and my heart rate sped up.

"I'm fine right here." I downed my drink, locking my phone back.

Tae's tongue slowly swiped over his top teeth and his eyes narrowed.

"I didn't ask you. I'm telling you to come with me really quick." The authority in his voice made my center throb.

"Oop," Aisha snickered while kissing on her nephew.

Gage laughed in the background as well.

My attention zeroed in on Tae. I hated how my body craved to be close to him. Although my mind had made the decision that we were done with him, the rest of me hadn't caught up.

"Brenna." This time his voice dropped into a husky octave.

A tingling sensation swarmed my body.

Pushing a heavy sigh out, I placed my phone back in my purse, rolled my eyes and stood up. Not bothering to speak, Tae nodded his head in the direction he wanted me to go.

I could hear Aisha and Gage talking behind me, but I didn't bother to listen to what was being said.

A few seconds later, Tae had caught up to me and grabbed me by the elbow, leading me out the hall to an empty part of the building.

The moment we were out of everyone's sight, he had me pinned up against the wall with his body pressed close to me.

His eyes were low as he glared at me.

My pulse raced in my throat. "Why you fucking playing with me?" His hand went to my side and sunk into me while the other laid flat on the wall above my head.

Just I was about to answer him, my words were cut off by his lips on mine and his tongue down my throat. My body instantly melted into him. Memories of our time together flashed through my mind causing the fire inside me to burn hotter. A moan fell from my mouth into his.

My arms wrapped around his neck and my body arched into him.

"I see I'ma have to remind you who the fuck I am," he growled against my mouth.

I jumped when his hand slipped under the dress I was wearing. His fingers brushed over my lower lips, which were only hidden by the thin thong I had on.

"I barely touched you and you wet as fuck." His thumb pressed against my sensitive clit making me whimper.

I always appreciated how in tune he was when it came to pleasing a woman. He may have been a hoe and wasn't trying to settle down, but he had learned how to properly handle a woman.

His mouth moved from my mouth to the corner of it, down to my chin, and eventually found my neck. He had now moved my thong to the side and was teasing my lower lips with his thick fingers.

I inhaled a sharp breath and closed my eyes, allowing my head to fall back as he sucked on my neck, tonguing it.

Moving my arms down until I gripped his toned arms, I mentally told myself I needed to stop this, but as always, my body was betraying me.

"I see someone missed me." He sucked roughly on my skin.

"We shouldn't be doing this," I forced out, yet my hips were moving against his fingers.

"I can't tell." I gasped when one of his fingers penetrated me, then another. Tae skillfully moved them in and out of me while still kissing my neck.

My stomach tightened when he found my spot and pushed up against it.

"I see some things ain't changed." My walls tightened around his fingers. He inserted a third and attacked my spot.

Tae pulled up and stared me in the face as he finger fucked me. Digging my fingers into his shoulders, I tried to fight it, but it was a sad attempt. The moment he made contact with my bud again, I was cumming.

"Just like that," he said huskily. His eyes were dark and pene- trating. "You keep trying to deny this shit like I don't know how to work this pussy better than any muthafucka you deal with."

I tried to speak, but my words got lodged in my throat. His

words almost had me cumming again because they were true. Tae sexed like he studied it for a living. He never half-assed it. I didn't know if it was just with me or in general, but I never had a reason to complain.

My eyes closed as I tried to gather myself.

Instead of waiting for me to form a sentence, Tae picked me up and dropped me down on his dick before I could protest. Another thing about Tae was he wasn't shy about where he had sex. While we both should have been on guard since his sister's wedding reception was filled with his family and friends just a few feet away, it was an afterthought. I always told Tae that he was an adrenaline junky. The thought of being caught by whoever excited him for whatever reason.

Just like I remembered, his dick filled my walls with ease, leaving no spot untouched.

Tae aggressively dug into me while I tried to contain my moans. My hold on him grew tight and my mouth parted as he tapped my spot over and over. His hands gripped my ass cheeks, spreading them and bringing me down on him roughly.

"That nigga fucking you like this, B?" Tae growled

Quickly I shook my head. I didn't know how Tae knew I was dealing with someone else, probably Aisha, but I didn't care. Sex with Randy was nice, but he didn't fuck me like Tae did. It was now that I realized how much I missed this.

"Ain't no nigga gone ever fuck you like this either." I cried out when he slammed me down on him. My walls tightened around his shaft.

Moving in, Tae took my mouth, biting my bottom lip and sucking on it sensually.

Fire spread through my body.

My heart slammed against my ribcage and my head began to spin.

"Don't stop, please don't stop," I begged, feeling myself about to cum again.

"I shouldn't even give you this nut," he gritted against my mouth. His strokes slowed but didn't let up.

I ignored his words and rode the wave of ecstasy he was bringing me.

"That a girl, let that shit go." He bit on my bottom lip again before kissing me.

My eyes squeezed shut as my body shook violently.

When my head fell back, Tae pressed his lips against the hollow part of my throat while still moving in and out of me.

"Tell me where you want this nut, B," he groaned, dragging his tongue down my skin.

"In me," I robotically responded.

"Fuck, I was hoping you said that."

My back pressed against the wall as Tae's head dropped forward and his dick jumped inside me.

Feeling his seeds coat my walls had me cumming again with him.

For a moment, neither of us spoke. All that could be heard between us was heavy breathing and our hearts pounding.

Slowly Tae removed himself from inside me. When I felt his dick withdraw, I snapped back into reality.

Panic shot through me.

"We shouldn't have done this!" I instantly pushed him away and shoved my dress down.

A hard glare formed on his face.

"I'm trying to move on. This isn't moving on!" I exclaimed out loud.

"Brenna, quit acting like you don't miss a nigga. I know that pussy do just by how she was just singing to me.

My eyes cut in his direction. "She was confused," I let him know.

A shiver shot through me, feeling our mixed juices run out of me.

"Bathroom," I muttered.

Not bothering to stick around, I rushed past Tae to find the ladies' room. This was why I stayed away from him. I knew that whenever I was around him, especially the two of us alone, my judgment would lapse and my pussy would end up wrapped around his good ass dick.

two

Devontae "Tae" King

"LOOK like all yo ass is good for is producing girls." I laughed, sitting back on Gage's couch as he held his newborn daughter. "You know they say a fuck boy gets his karma with daughters."

His eyes cut in my direction. "Shut yo punk ass up." His words caused me to laugh again. "A nigga was just meant to be a girl dad."

Sometimes it was still surreal to me that my best friend and little sister had kids together and were now married. When I first found out, I was pissed and ready to knock his damn head off. Aisha was my heart and there was nothing I wouldn't do for her. Knowing the type of nigga Gage was, I thought the two of them would be a bad mix, but I was proven wrong. Gage might have taken his time getting his shit together, but in the end, he did. I knew my sister and niece were happy, and that's all that mattered to me.

"Where's DJ?" He asked me.

"With Tia's worrisome ass." I chewed on the inside of my cheek. My son had just left my care after being with me for over a week. If I had it my way he would still be with me. Tia called me crying, saying I was trying to keep our son away from her and demanding I bring him home. Not wanting to hear her mouth, I did as she requested, but not before letting her know I was getting in back in a couple of days.

If I was being honest, I don't think Tia wanted to be a mom. She tried to use my son as something to hold over my head. Although I love my son, he wasn't supposed to happen. Shit with Tia and I got wild one night and the condom broke. I bought her a plan B, but instead of making sure she swallowed it, I stupidly trusted her to take it. When she came to me screaming she was pregnant, I waved her off, knowing I got her the pill. I was sure I wasn't the only nigga she was fucking, but fate had other plans. When the DNA test came back, I was the dad. I pushed my disappointment to the side and stepped up. I loved my son but hated his extra ass mama. Nothing satisfied her.

My son was going on six months, and Tia was always trying to get all this extra shit he didn't need. When I didn't hand over the money, she screamed that deadbeat bullshit. As long as I ensured my son had the essentials he needed, I didn't pay her complaints any attention.

"You thought about what we talked about?" He asked, laying Brooklyn down on the blanket next to him. She squirmed some and balled her body up, sleeping peacefully.

"I hate to even take it there, but it's looking like I might have to."

I had only known DJ was mine for a few months. In the beginning, Tia refused to give me a paternity test. In the short time since finding out, she has been a pain in my ass. My parents, sister, and Gage suggested I take her to court for custody. It was early but I could already see Tia didn't take being a mother seriously. She wanted to deal with our son when she felt like it and wanted me to hand her over money like it grew on trees. Although I wasn't broke, I wasn't rich either. I made good money as a personal trainer. Gage had even hooked me up with a few of his teammates who hired me for private sessions at their home gyms. I was comfortable and working on expanding my talent.

"If things don't get better, I say do it. We too fucking old to be dealing with baby mama drama." I nodded in agreeance.

"You can say that shit again."

I checked the time on my phone. I had to be at the gym for a session with a client in a couple of hours. Growing up, I played sports but enjoyed being in the gym and working out more. When I was stressed out or needed to clear my head, the first place I went to was the gym. It only made sense that I became a personal trainer.

Gage's front door opened and giggles could be heard throughout the room.

A few moments later, Aisha and Brenna stepped into the living room.

My eyes immediately locked on the warm, tan-skinned beauty in front of me. Instantly I noticed the change in her hair. She had cut her once shoulder-length tresses into a pixie cut that perfectly fit her heart-shaped face. I also noticed the chocolate brown color that now covered it.

"Hey y'all!" Aisha spoke, making her way to her husband.

First, she leaned down and pecked her daughter's cheek, then lifted her head to Gage's. My face balled up as the two kissed. I might accept them being together now, but I didn't want to see that shit.

"Where's my baby girl?" Gage asked, noticing Bailey was missing.

"She wanted to stay with my parents. They're going to drop her off later."

Gage nodded and looked over at Brenna. "Wassup, Brenna."

A small smile formed on her full, glossed lips. "Hey, Gage."

I knew she could feel my eyes burning into her, but she refused to meet my gaze. Since I dicked her down at the wedding she was back to avoiding me. Normally I wouldn't be bothered by it, but Brenna was different. She was someone I was really feeling and enjoyed being around. It fucked me up when she called it quits.

"You don't see anyone else?" I questioned Brenna.

She cut her sienna brown, jewel shaped eyes in my direction. "Hello, Devontae." Her voice was void of any emotion.

I chuckled and swiped my bottom lip with my thumb. "I see you on yo bullshit today." I bobbed my head.

"Can you two please not start today?" Aisha groaned, taking a seat next to Gage and laying her head on his chest while his arm enveloped her.

"Yo friend got a shitty ass attitude. Take that up with her." I lifted my shoulders and took a glance at my phone again.

My eyes squinted and jaw clenched. "This bitch, man," I groaned at a text from Tia, telling me she needed me to come get DJ.

"What's wrong?" Aisha asked.

Instead of answering, I stood up and exited the room to call Tia. She didn't take long to answer.

My brows furrowed together at the sounds of my son's cries in the background. "Yo, what the fuck is wrong with him?"

"He won't stop crying! That's what's wrong! I can't get him to stop, so you need to come get him!"

"Tia, you just got him back! Plus, I have clients later. I can't get him."

"You're his father, Tae! You need to make time for your son. All this crying is giving me a damn headache! Now either you can get him, or I'll take him to my parents. DJ, hush up!"

Her yelling at my son caused infuriated me. This was the shit I was talking about. Tia couldn't handle our son for more than a few days before she was calling and crying for me to pick him up or calling her parents to get him. "Aye, I'm on my way!" I hung up the phone without waiting for her to respond.

Running my hand down my face, I chewed the inside of my jaw as I stalked back into the living room.

"I gotta go," I told them before heading to the door.

"Is everything okay?" Aisha asked.

I was on my phone about to reach out to my clients for the evening. I would have to reschedule their appointments.

"Tia's stupid ass got DJ over there crying and can't calm him down. I'm about to go get him," I replied angrily.

"I thought you worked tonight?"

"I do, but I'ma have to reschedule my clients."

"Don't do that! Bring him over here."

Lifting my eyes from my phone, I looked at my sister. "I don't want to intrude on y'all."

Aisha rolled her eyes before giving me a hard glare. "As much as you helped out with Bailey, I owe you! Plus, I love my nephew. I don't know how many times I have to tell you watching him is no big deal."

"She's right. DJ is my little nigga. He be chillin,'" Gage agreed.

I sighed and allowed my shoulders to fall forward.

My family was more than willing to help out with my son, but I didn't like asking unless it was absolutely necessary. Aisha and Gage had Bailey and a newborn, so I didn't like pawning my son off on them. My parents were always willing too, but I tried not to burden them either.

DJ had a perfectly fine mom who was capable of keeping him on days I couldn't, but she always found a reason why she couldn't last longer than two or three days.

"I 'preciate you, sis."

She waved me off. "You just need to get full custody. Tia obviously doesn't want to be a mom. She hardly ever has him." My sister was right, but I didn't want to take my son from his mother, especially not at this early age. I knew how important it was for a baby to have his mother.

"I just told him the same thing. All that stupid shit she be on is for the birds."

Not bothering to respond to either of them, I turned my head and my attention landed on Brenna, who was smiling and texting on her phone. This time when she felt my eyes on her, she looked up at me.

Truthfully, I hated the space we were in. We didn't end on bad terms. I understood her not wanting to deal with a guy with kids, especially with the bullshit my baby mama be on, but since we stopped whatever we were doing, she made sure to steer clear of me.

My phone vibrated in my hand.

Baby mama from hell: *Where are you?? Hurry up!!!*

My grip tightened on my phone.

"I'll be back to drop him off." I stormed towards the door.

"Tae!" Aisha called out after me. "Make sure you get proof of how unfit she is."

Hurriedly, I nodded my head.

Tia was in for a rude awakening when I picked my son up. It was time we set some shit straight.

———

When I pulled up to Tia's house, I sat in my car for a few minutes. The car ride across town didn't soothe the anger building inside of me. Instead, it only caused my irritation to grow. It pained me that my son had to be subjected to the stupidity of his mother.

Rolling my neck between my shoulders, I turned my car off and finally stepped out.

As I approached Tia's front door, it was snatched open before I could even knock.

"It's about time you showed up!" Tia stood in front of me with her face made up, wearing a halter top and shorts. It looked like she was on her way out instead of trying to calm our son, who was now silent.

"Where's my son?" I pushed past her and made my way inside her house.

"He's sleeping." When I heard the door shut, I spun around glaring at her.

Her long weave was parted down the middle and hanging at her sides. Nails looked freshly done.

My jaw clenched tighter.

Staring at Tia reminded me why I didn't fuck with girls younger than me. They lacked the level of maturity I was used to with older women. Brenna and Tia were the only women younger I had dealt with since hitting twenty-five.

Sometimes I forgot that Tia was only twenty-two until I was in her presence. Her thick frame and fat ass had enticed me over the years. Even though she had a youthful face, Tia was stacked like a grown woman. She was an aspiring Instagram model that fed off attention.

Still, I couldn't blame it on her age because my sister had become a mother at 18, and she immediately stepped up to the plate. Tia was just stupid as hell.

Knowing if I spoke to her now, I might say some shit I'd regret, I turned and headed for my son's room. Walking through Tia's house, you wouldn't even know she had a kid. There were hardly any baby items throughout it.

Finally reaching my son's room, my anger skyrocketed. The foul smell coming from him caused my blood to boil. When I got to his crib, I noted the tear stains on his flushed cheeks, indicating she'd let him cry himself to sleep.

Biting the inside of his jaw, I moved the cover and my eyes bucked at the soiled diaper. It was obvious from the smell and size that he hadn't been changed recently, if at all today.

My jaw ached as I moved around the room looking for supplies to change my son's diaper. My heart ached thinking of him dealing with this since I left him in Tia's care.

Pushing a deep breath out, I took my phone and made sure I got some pictures of his nursery. The more I observed what was going on, the hotter my body became.

DJ shifted and whined as I changed him. His eyes fluttered open and a small cry left his mouth.

"It's okay, man. Daddy's here," I soothed him.

It took a few minutes, but when he realized I was here, his frown turned into a smile as coos left his mouth.

"Don't worry, son. I'm taking you away from this dumb bitch." I hated to speak about Tia like that in front of him, but I couldn't think of any other way to address her.

My stomach flipped when I noticed the irritation and chaffing around his private area and butt. I looked around and wasn't surprised when I didn't see any ointment.

I cleaned him up and changed him with what I was able to scrounge up. I kissed my son's cheek once I had him in my arms.

"Let's go, son." I didn't need shit from Tia. I had everything my son needed with me, including a car seat.

When I got into the living room, Tia was on the phone laughing and talking. "Yeah, girl, DJ is leaving with his daddy. I'll be there in a minute."

"Hang up the phone," I growled, laying my son on the couch beside her.

Her eyes shifted up to me before they rolled and landed back on her phone.

"Girl, baby daddy wanna talk to me. I'll see you in a few."

Tia hung the phone up.

I tried to keep my temper under wraps. Another reason I loved working out was that any aggression I felt, getting my heart racing and adrenaline running in the gym always helped.

"Let me holla at you." I nodded my head towards the back of her house.

I didn't want to argue in front of our son.

Tia smacked her lips and followed me out of the living room to the hallway. Once it was just us, I turned and gripped her by the neck and slammed her into the wall.

Her eyes bucked and her mouth dropped.

I wasn't choking her, but I had a firm grip on her. Putting my hands on a woman wasn't me, and my mama and daddy would beat my ass if they saw me now, but it was needed at this moment.

"What the fuck is wrong with you!" My voice boomed in the shallow walkway. "My fucking son looked and smelled like shit when I got here. Not to mention you let him cry himself to sleep!"

"Let me go!" She yelled, clawing at my hands.

My grip on her neck tightened and my eyes narrowed. "You won't see my son anymore. I tried to play nice and let you be in his life, but that shits a wrap. Until you get your shit together and show me you deserve to be a mother, he'll be in my care."

"Ta-tae," she struggled to get out.

"I'm not fucking done." My voice dropped. Tia's mouth snapped shut. "If you want to be around my son, then you need to get your shit together, Tia. I'm tired of being the nice guy. Don't call my fucking phone until you're ready to be a mother!"

I gave her one final hard glare before releasing her and letting her fall. She was gasping for air as if I had choked her out, but I knew I hadn't and didn't pay her any attention.

"Fuck you, Tae! You can't take my son!" she sputtered.

I didn't have a response for her. Tia wasn't fit to be a mother, and I wouldn't allow my son to keep suffering under her care.

Walking back to her couch, I smiled when I laid eyes on my son. He was a naturally happy baby. He hardly cried or fussed. Most of the time, if you gave him a toy, he was good.

"C'mon, little man. Let's get the fuck outta here." I swooped him up.

He babbled his baby talk and reached for my face.

I could never regret my son. It was like being a father came naturally to me. I feared that I might mess up, but whenever I looked at my son and saw how happy he was, those thoughts went out the window. However, I do regret ever spilling my seeds inside his damn mama.

three

Brenna

"WHAT'S ON YOUR MIND?" Randy asked me with my feet in his hands.

Glancing over at him, I snapped out of my thoughts and gave him a small smile. "Just thinking."

"Anything you want to share?"

My eyes scanned over his coffee-colored face for a second, then focused on his pecan, almond-shaped orbs.

Shaking my head, I sighed. "Since Aisha's wedding, I've been getting a lot of inquiries for events. Planning a famous basketball player's wedding was just what my career needed." I told a half-truth.

Business has been going well since the wedding. Multiple people have inquired about Aisha and Gage's wedding planner, and my name was even mentioned in the credits during the special. It had been a blessing, especially since I've only been open for business for a year now.

Still, that wasn't what was on my mind. I couldn't get what happened with Tae the other day out of my head. Aisha had previously mentioned how he had issues with his child's mom but seeing it firsthand was different.

When he returned to Aisha's after getting his son, you could practically see the steam coming out of his head. He told us about the state his son was in once he got to Tia's house, and Aisha instantly got hype. I couldn't deny I did as well. I may not want kids, but that didn't mean I wanted any of them to be mistreated.

Tae's baby mama sounded like she needed her ass whooped.

Hearing the pain and disgust in Tae's voice as he spoke pained me. Tae and I might not have been a thing anymore, but I still cared about him. He irritated me a lot of the time, but that didn't mean I wanted to see him in disarray.

He didn't stay around long after that, leaving to set out to the gym. I found myself wanting to comfort him but refrained.

"You know if you need any help, I got you," Randy offered, bringing my attention back to him.

My smile grew. "I know. Thank you."

Randy owned a few high-end housing developments, including Sunset Developments and a new build in *New Haven*.

He dropped my left foot and picked up the other one, kneading it.

I met Randy while leaving the bank one day. He was entering and held the door open for me. He ended up stopping me and asking me out.

Randy was handsome and dressed nice He kept the goatee around his lips short and groomed. Hair freshly lined up and cut low, and he smelled good. I didn't hesitate to give him my number.

That was a few months ago, and I had been enjoying his company. Randy was sweet, and I enjoyed the time we spent together. He always made sure to give me his full attention when we were together and was respectful. He told me that he was raised by his grandma and mother. They made sure he grew up respecting women and knowing how to take care of them.

"I have a business meeting down in Miami coming up. I'm

looking at some land down there. I was wondering if you wanted to come with me. Maybe a getaway is what you need."

Bringing my bottom lip between my teeth, I thought his offer over. It sounded nice.

"I don't know. With business picking up, I might be busy," I smirked.

He chuckled.

A low moan left my mouth when he applied pressure on the center of the bottom of my foot. "Already leaving us small folks behind, huh?"

Trying to fight my smile from growing, I removed my feet from his hands and leaned forward.

"Never," I mumbled. Leaning in, I pressed my lips against his.

His long arms wrapped around me and his hands gripped my ass cheeks, pulling me into his lap.

I needed to meet with a client in a few hours to go over details for the birthday party he's throwing for his wife. Until then, I was going to allow Randy to work some stress out of me.

———

I used the back of my hand to wipe the sweat from my brows as I stepped off the treadmill. I wasn't big on working out, but I tried to stop by the gym a least twice a week to attempt to stay in some kind of shape.

"*I'm F-R-E-E fuck nigga free,*" I rapped along to the song playing through my AirPods. Working out to ratchet music always motivated me.

Making my way to the dressing room, I went to the locker that housed my drawstring bag. I had been here for a little over an hour. Today I just wanted to run on the treadmill, so there was no point in being here any longer.

Facing the mirror, I brushed my hand through the few hairs stuck to my forehead. This haircut was different, but I liked it. My hair was so unhealthy before the cut that I decided to do the big chop and try going natural. Marsha, the owner of *Crown Studio Hair Salon*, had also hooked me up with her hair care line. So far, my hair was loving it.

After wetting a paper towel and wiping my face, I headed for the door.

Subconsciously my eyes scanned the gym, looking for *him*. For months I had been able to ignore my urges for Tae and continue on as if we never had anything— until Aisha's wedding. Feeling him inside me again had unlocked the very door I had tried to close and throw away the key. Now I found myself thinking about him again. The only way I could not give in to those feelings was when I was being a bitch to him. I hated that Tae was such a hard presence to forget.

My heart stuttered in my chest when I laid eyes on *him*. He was sitting behind the front desk on his phone. When I first arrived at the gym, he was in the middle of training a client, so I didn't get to speak to him.

Slowly, I made my way toward the front desk. When I got close, I noticed his large, toned arms in his cut-off shirt. Tae didn't have many tattoos, just the ones on his neck and a rose bush on his upper right arm with his mom, sister, and Bailey's name engraved in them.

"Hey," I leaned on the counter and spoke.

Tae's head lifted and his eyes focused on me. An emotionless expression rested on his face. For some reason, the look he was giving me caused my heart to race and goosebumps to prickle my skin.

"Wassup." The coldness in his voice almost made me turn away.

His hooded eyes seemed darker than normal.

"I just wanted to check on you. I know the other day you were going through a lot with your son and his mom."

His face remained blank.

Tae's eyes peered into me as if he were looking through me. His jaw clenched for a moment.

He didn't respond right away. The sounds of weights clanking together, low grunts, and chatter could be heard around us. Every so often, someone would scan their membership card before heading towards the main floor.

"You don't even fuck with my son, so why do you care?" His words, as well as his tone, caught me off guard. My head cocked back as if he had struck me.

Standing up straight, I stared at him with my mouth turned upside down. "What are you talking about? I never said that."

"You didn't have to. I got enough shit going on. I don't need your fake love or concern."

I scoffed. "Fake love and concern? I'm not faking shit. I'm genuinely concerned."

"Like I said, I don't need no fake concern. You can keep that shit." Tae picked his phone back up. I suppose it was his way of dismissing me.

My heart was heavy in my chest. Back and forth bantering with Tae was normal but never had he spoken to me so emotionless and cold. It caused my whole body to grow cold and my heart to ache.

I blinked a few times, wondering if I should press the issue or give up. Gnawing on my bottom lip, I decided to leave and give him space.

You don't even fuck with my son, so why do you care? His words rung through my head as I walked away. Each step I took caused my stomach to churn.

Never had I said I didn't fuck with Tae's son. Hell, I had only been around the little boy a handful of times and could admit he was a sweet kid. Ending things with Tae didn't mean I didn't fuck with his son. I just wasn't the motherly type. I enjoyed my me time, and I was selfish as hell with my time. I knew if a kid came into play, I would have to share my time, and as selfish as it sounded, I didn't want to do that. When I started feeling someone, I became needy and clingy, too. My feelings for Tae were growing stronger the longer I was around him, and I knew what that meant.

I would never ask Devontae to choose between his son and me, so I took myself out of the equation.

Suddenly my blood grew hot and my stomach flipped.

Spinning around, I turned and stormed back to the desk. When I slammed my hands on top of it, Tae's head shot up. His forehead creased, brows bunched together, and his mouth turned into a frown.

"For your information, I never said I didn't fuck with your son. If I didn't give a damn, I wouldn't have asked you how you were doing. Don't take whatever bullshit your baby mama is putting you through out on me because I don't deserve it!"

Turning around, I marched to the door without giving him a chance to respond.

This was another reason I removed myself from whatever Tae and I were doing. I wasn't built for baby mama drama. I liked to live a peaceful life. The only stress I accepted was from my business.

Making my way across the parking lot, I approached my small SUV.

Devontae had just left a bad taste in my mouth. My eyes traveled back to the gym, and I sat there staring at the entrance for a little longer. I wish I could brush Tae off like I had done other guys in the past, but I couldn't. He had imprinted himself in me.

Sighing, I rolled my eyes and pressed the push button to start my car. My car lit up and my phone connected. FNF blared through the speakers.

"Run that back," I muttered, restarting the song before throwing my truck in drive.

The last thing I was going to do was let Devontae King get me out my hookup.

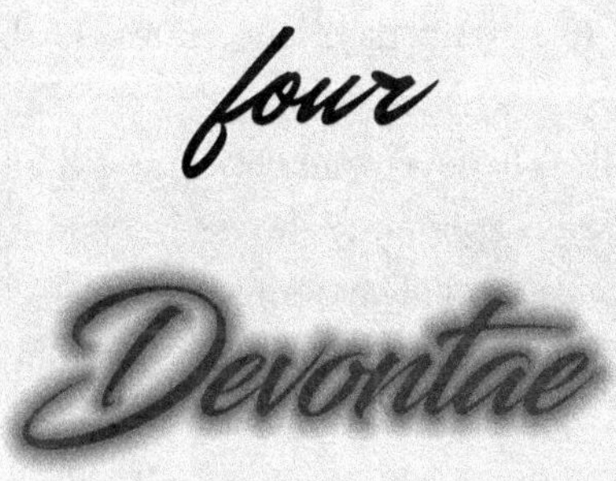

"SO, I see you have a degree in childcare and early childhood development, and you're certified in CPR." Taking my eyes off the paperwork, I glanced at Kaia, the potential babysitter I was interviewing.

Since it was looking like I was going to have DJ full time, I decided to hire someone to help. I didn't want to always rely on my family to stop what they were doing to assist me. My hours at the gym used to be all over, but now that I had my son, I was creating a set schedule for my clients.

Kaia grinned brightly at me. "Yes, I worked at a daycare for two years until I left."

"And why did you leave?" I raised an eyebrow.

"I wanted to get into private childcare. I loved working at the daycare but prefer to work with individual kids as a nanny."

Nodding my head, I read over the papers again. Kaia was the fourth sitter I had interviewed today, and out of all of them, she was the one I was feeling the most. She had several references, including from the previous daycare she spoke on. She didn't hesitate to answer every question I asked, and her smile was genuine.

Kaia was twenty-six and had a lot of background in childcare already.

"My schedule is kind of all over right now, but I'm working on getting it set to certain days and times. Is that an issue?" I asked her.

"No, not at all. Whenever you need me, I'll be available."

Kaia's smile was captivating. It was big and welcoming.

I gave her a once-over. The orange sun dress she wore looked good against her golden skin. Her hair was pulled into a ponytail on her neck.

I nodded. "A'right, I just need to call a few of these references, but I think I've made up my mind." I laid the papers on my lap. "You busy tonight?" I tilted my head to the side.

"No, I'm not." Her voice was soft and bubbly.

"I'm supposed to meet up with a few people later on. We can do a trial run and see how things go."

"Sounds good to me!" Her smile widened and eyes lit up.

I didn't want just anyone around my son. With the bullshit his mom already put him through, I didn't want to subject him to anyone else that would mistreat him. Kaia didn't give off any vibes that I shouldn't trust her. Her background was clean and she was highly certified for the job.

If tonight went well, then I would consider hiring her full-time.

———

"What's up with you? You been in your head since we got here," Gage inquired.

"Yeah, normally you would be talking shit, but you've barely spoken and *you're winning*," Elijah followed up.

My eyes went to the pool table as I brought my Silver Shadow's Beer to my lips. Elijah had released a new flavor in honor of summer, and this was the first time I tasted it.

"Just thinking about some shit." Setting my beer bottle down, I reached for my phone and pulled up the cameras in my house. Being that Kaia was a stranger, I was being more cautious with my son. I had installed nanny cameras throughout my house to peek in when needed. She had just placed the interactive mat Aisha had gotten for DJ on the ground and then walked over to the couch where he was laying down. Picking him up, she walked over to the mat and the two laid on it.

DJ seemed to be fine and was smiling and doing his typical baby babble.

"Who dat?" Glancing over my shoulder, I saw Elijah had moved closer.

"DJ's babysitter."

He whistled. "Shit, they making them like that? Now maybe I need to get me a kid."

Ignoring him, I closed out the app and slid my phone in my pocket.

"You fucking your nanny?" Elijah's question caused my head to snap in his direction and my brows to bunch together.

"What? Hell nah. I don't even know if I'ma keep her. This is just a trial run."

"Shit, with her looking like that, I would keep her."

I shook my head. Kaia was attractive. She was slim but had a cute shape. Her round face, big doe eyes, and full pouty lips gave her an innocent look.

"I ain't even going in that direction. I just need her to watch my son when I'm not around, and that's it."

"His ass still stuck on Brenna's ass anyway," Gage chimed in, chuckling.

My eyes cut to him. "Ain't no one thinking about that girl."

One corner of Gage's mouth rose. "Then why yo ass on a dry spell right now?" He grinned.

Waving him off, I walked back to the pool table to take my turn. "I have enough problems with my baby mama. Her ass got me being more cautious who I put my dick in." I lined my stick up and pushed it forward.

After how I handled Brenna the other day, I knew she wasn't fucking with me anyway. I had been in a bad mood since getting my son from Tia. The state I found him in had been heavy on my mind. I knew I owed her an apology, especially after she tore into me. It lowkey made my dick hard.

"You ain't lying about that. Gage got lucky with your sister, but I know I don't even want kids or a baby mama after seeing your situation."

I shook my head and stood up after I missed the shot. "Nah, having a kid is great. It's the baby mama part that's a pain in the ass."

"Aisha's a rare breed. I wish I would have known that shit back then." For a moment, Gage seemed to zone out and get lost in his head.

"All that matters is that you have your shit together now."

"Gage! Can we get your autograph?" Two young looking girls approached us, smiling widely at Gage.

Amusement filled me seeing a basketball in one of their hands. "Sure." He nodded at them and grabbed the black permeant maker.

I wasn't shocked that he was approached.

Most of the time, no one paid Gage any attention. He didn't walk around with a big ego when he was home. He was just like everyone else and normally wanted to stay lowkey, a 360 from the person he used to be. I know my sister and the struggles he went through over the past couple of years had a lot to do with that. Both humbled him.

Gage was a frequent patron at *Priority Play*. If you wanted to see him, this was where you could mostly find him, and he didn't mind interacting with his fans.

Once the girls got pictures they walked away giggling.

"Does that ever get old?" Elijah asked him.

Gage walked up to the table, preparing his shot. "Nah. I mean, you know a nigga loves attention. I've just toned it down. I'm cool as long as they don't approach me when my kids or wife are with me. This city welcomed me back home with open arms after all the shit I went through. I'll forever be grateful to them." He hit the white ball.

That I agreed with. When Gage announced he was coming back to Butter Ridge Falls to play basketball, everyone was excited. Even with his injury, he was still playing like a champ. If anything, that only made him go harder.

"Back to you, Tae. You know Aisha and yo mama gone be pissed you hired a nanny, right?"

This time I smirked. "Yeah, I know." My hand ran over my head.

I was raised to handle my responsibilities. I laid down with Tia and created our son, and it was up to me to make sure he was good. Putting him off on my family all the time didn't sit well with me.

"You ready for the season to start?" Gage had one more month of off-season before basketball resumed.

"Hell yeah! I'm coming for the ship this year. It's been snatched out of my hands too many times."

I nodded.

I was sure Gage would have gotten a ring if he hadn't been injured before the playoffs. His injury put his team in a bad place because he was the franchise player. Last year he was coming fresh off his injury, but this year The Titans were stacked, and I knew a ring was coming this way.

A night out with the guys is what I needed. It had been a while since we got together. Life had been taking us all in different directions, but we always tried to link at least once a month. The only person missing was Wes, who was in medical school.

It was my turn now, and I focused on making my shot this time. I was trying not to worry so much and enjoy the night out.

———

Stepping into Mama's, I walked up to the counter to order my food. My parents had all their grandkids this morning, giving me some time to myself.

Things with Kaia seemed to go well last night. When I got home, DJ was sleeping peacefully in his crib. She had cleaned up and was sitting on the couch watching TV. Seeing that everything looked intact, I paid and thanked her before sending her on her way.

Kaia seemed like a good fit, and DJ liked her. I called some of her references and got helpful feedback from them. She seemed like a safe bet.

My eyes traveled around the restaurant and stopped when I noticed Brenna.

Without thinking, I made my way to her table. She had her iPad, some folders, and papers spread out on the table, along with a plate of pancakes, eggs, and sausage.

"I see breakfast is still your favorite meal," I spoke up, gaining her attention.

She looked up at me with squinted eyes and bunched brows. Her mouth was pressed in a straight line. It was obvious she was still upset about what happened at the gym.

I scanned the table over, noting it was work-related papers on it. "Can I sit?" I nodded towards the empty booth seat across from her.

"If you came to bite my head off some more then-"

I shook my head. "I didn't."

Hesitancy still rested on her face, but she nodded her head. I didn't miss how tense her shoulders looked either.

Sliding in the booth, I watched as she went back to her work. Brenna often mentioned how she was a morning person and got her best work done first thing in the morning.

"I owe you an apology," I started the conversation, making her head snap up at me. "I was still in a fucked up mood from the shit that happened with Tia, and I took it out on you. I shouldn't have done that."

Her lips tucked in her mouth for a moment. She tapped the pen in her hand against the table and stared at me.

"I don't hate your son and never said I did," she finally responded after what seemed like forever.

I bit the inside of my jaw, hating that I even let some shit like that come out of my mouth. I knew Brenna. Even before we started fucking, I knew her. I was aware that she would never have any malicious feelings in her heart toward a baby, especially towards my son.

"I know." I ran my hand over my head and scratched my jaw. "I shouldn't have said no shit like that to you."

My arms rested on the table and I balled my hands into a fist.

"You aren't a fucked up female, Brenna. You're actually pretty dope." Her cheeks tinted red at that comment. "I've seen you with both of my sister's kids and you're good with them. You love them, so I know you don't hate kids. I just don't understand why me having a kid is such a big issue to you."

I wanted Brenna, and I wasn't afraid to admit it.

Things with her were easy and came naturally. She was younger than me, but the bond the two of us built had me looking past that. Plus, Brenna didn't carry herself like she was younger than me. She was on her shit and made sure she handled her business. That shit was sexy as hell to me.

For a moment, her eyes dropped. When she looked back at me, her mouth was twisted to the side, and she was tapping her pen against the table again.

"Simple. I enjoy being the center of attention in my nigga's eye. I'm used to being able to move as we please without considering anyone else. I wanna be spoiled, and I can get clingy. I want my time to be my time, and I don't like sharing. I have no issue with Aisha's kids because I can give them back and don't have to be responsible for them. With your son, it means everything I want and crave, I have to share and split." She paused for a moment and swiped her tongue over her lips. "Why do you think you never heard me speak on kids? They need a lot of time and attention I'm not willing to give right now." She spoke lowly. Her eyes never left mine.

Pulling the corner of my bottom lip between my teeth, I took a moment to go over her words.

"I think that's bullshit," I said, causing her eyes to widen in surprise.

"What?"

"You heard me." I shrugged. "Just because a nigga has a kid doesn't mean your needs would be neglected. Being concerned about whether you would get enough attention is valid, but it's not something you need to worry about. A nigga gone make time for what or who he wants, period. Just because a kid is in the mix now doesn't mean that changes. Yeah, some things gone have to be adjusted and altered, but that doesn't mean anything. Truthfully, I can see you being a great mother, just by how you are with my nieces. I know when it comes to them, you would do anything."

"Tae, here's your food." Ginger, one of the waitresses, brought me my to-go order. She grinned widely as she sat my bag on the table.

"Appreciate it, Ging." I nodded at her.

Blushing, she bobbed her head and turned to leave.

My attention went back to Brenna, who was mugging Ginger. That made me laugh.

"Stop looking at her like that."

"Why did she come over here all bubbly?"

Chuckling again, I shook my head. "We went to school together. She's good people, chill."

Brenna looked at me and rolled her eyes. "If you say so." She picked up her orange juice and took a sip.

This wasn't the first time I saw Brenna's jealous side. It always gave me an ego boost, if I was being honest.

Licking my lips, I shook all those thoughts from my head and got back to the topic at hand. "You're Bailey and Brooklyn's God mom. If anything happens to their parents, you're next in line to get them. My sister wouldn't have done that if she didn't trust you would step up in her place and be who they need you to be. You're selling yourself short, and I think you need to get out of that mindset. Not wanting kids is cool. I didn't think I wanted them at first either, but now I have my son, and I wouldn't trade that for anything."

"I miss you, B." I reached over and grabbed her free hand. "I hear everything you're saying, but that doesn't take away from the fact that I miss you, and I know you miss a nigga too. I'm not trying to force my son into your life or force you to be a stepmother, but I don't want you to just give up because I now have a kid. We've known each other for years, and knowing the type of person you are, I know that you're selling yourself short." Gripping her hand for a second, I let it go and prepared to leave.

Brenna was staring at me silently, which was cool. I wasn't going to force myself back into her life or make her do something she didn't want to do. I just wanted her to see where I was coming from. Her doubts were valid, but I believed she was overthinking things more than anything.

I had fallen for Brenna. I don't know when, but I did. We started out just having sex, which turned into late night meets and sleepovers. She was a sneaky link that was never supposed to go beyond the bedroom. Once my sister found out about us, all that went out the window. No longer having to sneak around felt good.

Being alone with Brenna taught me a lot about her, more than I had learned in all the years I'd known her. I enjoyed seeing that side of her, and I wanted to continue learning more if she would let me.

five

Brenna

"HEY!" My little sister entered the living room and plopped down on the couch next to me.

Taking my attention off my iPad momentarily, I stared up at her. My sister was a smaller version of me. She was nineteen but looked just like me. When we were out together we were often mistaken for twins. The only difference is she got our mom's honey, almond-shaped eyes.

"What are you doing here?" She asked as I went back to my iPad. I was creating a digital mockup of a party I had coming up next week. I wanted to make sure everything looked good for me to send to the client.

"Daddy's washing my car," I told her while moving a few things around on the iPad.

"I should have known," she snickered.

"What does that mean?" I side eyed her.

She shook her head. "Just that every time you come over, you put him to work." This time I snickered.

"Hey, why pay someone to clean my car when I have a daddy that does it for free?"

"You're right about that. He just did mine yesterday." She laughed and pulled her phone out.

"Mommy called me this morning. Are you going to Aunt Quinn's birthday gathering?"

My face instantly balled up. "Absolutely not."

Raven giggled. "I told her you were going to say no."

Lifting one corner of my mouth, I eyed my tablet, making sure I approved of everything. "Aunt Quinn always got some shit going on. I'm not about to go over there and drama pops off not even an hour into the event."

I loved my mom's people, but her sisters Quinn and Jade were always in some bullshit. Quinn more than Jade. She still acted like she was in her 20s and couldn't accept that she was damn near fifty."

"Mommy said she's going for entertainment." I shook my head.

My mom was a lot more toned down than her sisters. She was the oldest of the three. Jade was the middle child, and Quinn the youngest.

"Are you going?" I emailed the digital mockup, locked my iPad, and gave my sister my attention.

She shrugged. "I work that morning, so it all depends on how I feel afterward. Plus, I need to study for this math test I have coming up." Raven was an intern at *Issa Vibe* magazine. Her goal was to be a full-time journalist. She was in school for journalism and communication.

"Yeah, you have fun with that." I waved her off.

A few seconds later, our dad walked into the living room. "You need to stop letting your gas get so damn low. I don't know how many times I've told you that," he fussed at me.

I fought back my laugh. "I planned to stop at the gas station when I left here."

He waved me off. "I already took it to the gas station and filled it up." This time I did smile.

I knew my daddy wouldn't let me leave here without a full tank; it was one of the reasons I waited. Flex Tucker was one of a kind. My daddy made sure my sister and I never wanted for anything. He was partially to blame for my spoiled and selfish behavior. He had set the bar high for the man I settled down with.

He looked good for his age too. Almost 50 years old, he was still in shape and took good care of himself. He had a few spots of grey in his short beard and had shaved his head bald a few years ago. Still, his cinnamon-colored skin had no wrinkles or blemishes.

"Thank you, daddy! You're the best!" I grinned and batted my lashes.

"Don't bullshit me, Brenna. I know yo ass purposely be letting your tank get low so I'll fill it up."

"Busted!" Raven laughed, and I couldn't help but join in.

"That is not true," I lied.

He narrowed his eyes. "Yeah, a'right. You can lie to them niggas you be dealing with but not me. It's cool though. I don't mind as long as I know you won't be somewhere stranded on the side of the road."

"Y'all hungry? I was thinking of heading to Chase's and grabbing something to eat."

"Your treat?" We both asked at the same time.

My dad chuckled lowly and shook his head. "Y'all think I'm made of money?"

"Kind of," Raven retorted.

Again, he chuckled. "My treat, girls."

That made me happy. I was wondering what I was going to eat today, but now that my dad had offered to feed me, I didn't have to anymore.

———

"Shit, I forgot what it felt like to go out!" Aisha spoke, taking a hit of the hookah. We had managed to make it to Happy Hour Thursdays at *Blue Smoke*.

"I know mommy and wife life been taking you by storm." I sipped on my Blue Muthafucka and bobbed my head to the music.

Aisha blew the smoke out and swayed to the music. "You're right. I forgot how much work a newborn was. This time Gage is there and he's so hands on. Bailey keeps me on my toes too. She wants to join so many different things, which is great. Along with running *A&B Prints* and finding time to spend with Gage before his season starts, it's a lot at times."

A small smile formed on my face. "You handle it all with ease though. It's like you were made for this life."

Aisha giggled. "I don't know about that, but I'm making it work," she downplayed.

I grabbed my wand and pulled on it, inhaling the watermelon berry flavor we had ordered.

"What about you? How are things going?" Aisha focused on me with her head slightly tilted.

I shrugged my shoulders. "Things are good, I guess. Since your wedding business has been booming, which is a blessing, and I have you to thank for it."

"Girl!" She pushed a breath out and waved her hand. "I didn't do anything but hire you. You're the one that put everything together. After I kicked that stupid ass planner the network originally had out of the picture, it was your show."

My cheeks heated and my heart swelled. "Still, you gave me a chance. It was my first time working on the actual wedding and not just the reception, and you trusted me. Since then, my inquires have been out the roof."

I ended up passing on Randy's offer to go to Miami with him because I had too much work piling up on me. With it just being me, I couldn't afford to take off right now.

"I'm proud of you. I know how scared you were to quit your job and take on your business full-time but look at you! You're killing it!"

I swallowed hard and fought not to get emotional. I had built my savings up enough that I felt comfortable and took a leap of faith. I'm just glad it all worked out.

"Thank you, friend."

She picked her drink up and took a sip. I was shocked she was drinking since she was breastfeeding, but she stated she would pump and dump.

"What about everything else? How are you and what's his name?"

"Randy."

"Randy, that's it!" She nodded. "How are things between you two?"

I swirled the drink around in my glass and brought my eyes down to it. Crossing my legs at the knee, I moved my foot side to side.

"We're good."

She gave me a curious look. "But?"

"But?"

"There's more you want to say. I know you, Brenna. What's up?"

Smiling softly, I shook my head and stared out at the dance floor. "That's it, there is no but. Randy and I are good and there's nothing else to tell. He's a great guy, amazing honestly, but there's nothing about what we have going on to brag about."

I swallowed hard and downed the rest of my drink.

Randy would make any girl happy, and I know he's a catch, but our relationship lacked sparks. It was more so on me than Randy. I found myself holding back from him.

"You haven't brought him around."

I nodded my head in agreeance. "Because I don't know if we're going to last."

There was no reason to entangle Randy in my world any further if nothing would come of us.

"Have you spoken to my brother?"

My stomach fluttered. "Uh, yeah, I saw him the other day." I shifted my eyes back to the dance floor.

What Tae said to me at *Mama's* had been sitting on my chest since he left my table. His words threw me completely off.

"Why did you make me the girls' God mom?" I asked suddenly.

Aisha's face twisted in confusion. "What do you mean? You're my best friend."

"But I mean deeper than that. A Godparent is like a backup parent if something happens to the original."

"Yeah, so." She shrugged.

"So, why me?"

"Why not you?" She frowned deeply. "I know my family will be more than willing to step up and take care of my kids, if necessary, but I also know you would too. They love you and love them. You would treat them like they're yours, and I know they would be well cared for."

"I don't know what to do about Tae."

"Meaning?"

With a soft grin, I turned to face my friend since childhood. It was awkward talking to her about my relationship with her brother, but I was glad she was open enough to allow me to vent. I know it was weird for her to hear about her best friend and her brother, but she never objected to it. Although she was upset when she first found out— because we kept it a secret, she has been supportive ever since. We never put her in the middle of things, but I was thankful for her being a listening ear.

"Him being a dad now. I never dealt with a guy with kids. Honestly, they turned me off. Sharing my person with a kid wasn't on the list for me, but I don't know. With Tae, it's differ-ent." I shook my head, feeling a stirring forming in my stomach.

"I ended things between us, but sometimes I wonder if I jumped the gun. You know how impulsive I can be at times."

Aisha didn't respond right away. Her eyes bore into me and her face was expressionless. It was actually scary because she looked like her brother right now.

"My brother is a good dude and even greater father," she started. "He's not perfect, but one thing I will say about him is he has the biggest heart I've seen. He's a natural giver and nurturer. My whole life he's always been in my corner. I know you've mentioned why you decided to end things, but maybe him having a kid isn't the real reason."

My brows knitted together. "What do you mean?"

"I mean, what if you were just hurt that Tae had a baby with someone else? I know you two weren't in an actual relationship, but you were involved on more than just a hookup level. You stopped dealing with him before you even knew if the kid was his. Maybe you subconsciously pushed him away so that you didn't have to face that hurt, and you used him becoming a dad as the reason."

I contemplated Aisha's words and processed them.

Was she right?

Did I really push Tae away because I was more hurt that he had a child with someone else and not because he had become a dad overnight?

six

Devontae

STARING DOWN AT MY PHONE, I shook my head as I stopped on a post on *InstaFlik* of Tia showing her ass. The latest pictures she posted were her half naked and shaking her ass. She and her friends were drinking and smoking around a group of niggas.

I could instantly feel a headache forming.

It had been a week since I got my son from her, and she hadn't called for him or asked about him. Seeing her go on as if she didn't have a child pissed me off and only pushed me to go the legal route to protect my son from her.

Licking my lips, I logged out of the app and climbed out of my car. Going to my back seat, I couldn't help but smile as I stared down at my son. His eyes were wide and bright. The moment he saw me he cheesed and started his baby jibberish while flailing his arms around.

"A'right, big man. Let's go see your grandparents." My hand went across the top of his head. His hair was thick already with tight curls.

Unhooking him out of his seat, I grabbed his diaper bag before heading to my parents' door.

As soon as I stepped inside the house, I felt a sense of calmness fill me. That's what my parents' house always did for me. It was a safe space. No matter what I had going on, I knew I could always look to my parents when needed.

I found my mom and dad in the living room, watching something on the TV.

"Wassup y'all," I spoke, walking deeper into the room.

"Hey son," my dad greeted me, but my mom turned her nose up.

"Hand me my grandson," my mom demanded.

Smirking, I did as she said. "Nice to see you too, beautiful."

I took a seat on the opposite couch. "I'm surprised you brought my grandson and didn't leave him with his *babysitter.*" My mom spoke if she had tasted something bad.

I chuckled. "You still upset I hired a sitter?"

My mom tickled DJ's stomach and he squealed in laughter. "I just don't understand why you would hire a stranger to watch DJ when your father and I are right here." She gave me an intense glare.

"Mom," I groaned. "I told you it was nothing personal. I just don't want you guys to be forced to deal with DJ all the time. Even though I'm working on implementing a set schedule, my work hours are still up and down. You both have lives."

My mom pushed out a heavy breath. "That's nonsense."

"I understand where you're coming from, Tae, but it was no problem. You know me and your mother love spending time with our grandkids."

"It's not like you guys will never babysit. I just thought it would be easier to have someone with open availability." My eyes went to my son, who was still smiling and babbling to my mom.

"I'm proud of you, Tae. I know you were thrown into fatherhood unexpectedly, but you're doing an amazing job," my mom suddenly told me.

"Your mom is right, son. You basically became a full-time parent overnight, but you haven't complained once."

I lifted my shoulders as if it wasn't a big deal. "I love my son. He deserves at least one parent that gives a damn about him."

Just the thought of Tia caused my blood to boil. "I'm going to reach out to a lawyer to file for full custody."

Both my parents gave me their full attention. "Are you sure? That's a big step."

I nodded and focused on DJ again. He was starting to grow fussy.

Going into his diaper bag, I grabbed the bottle I had made before leaving my house and leaned over, handing it to my mom.

"Tia doesn't want to be a mom. She's out here doing whatever she wants, not even bothering to check on him. Then I keep thinking about the state I found him in last week, and I can't allow him to keep getting subjected to that." My hands balled into fists.

"I have a friend whose daughter specializes in family law. I'll send you her number," my dad informed me.

"Thanks."

DJ ended up falling asleep shortly after my mom gave him his bottle. She cradled him in her arms and rocked him gently.

"By the way, I set up a photo shoot for the kids at *Gray Lens Co.* I bought outfits for the three of them too," my mom told me.

"Just send me the date and we'll be there."

Pulling my phone out, I went to my scheduling app for the gym. I had a light schedule this week. I was working with some of Gage's teammates to help them prepare for the upcoming season, so I did a light load for the next couple of weeks. The rates they were paying me more than made up for it.

I stayed around my parents' house a little longer before finally gathering my son and heading out.

When I got in the car, I received a message from my dad. It was the number of the lawyer he mentioned.

Diya Sands.

I called the number before pulling out of the driveway, leaving a message when she didn't answer.

Hopefully, she was good at her job and could help me. My eyes went to my review mirror and landed on my son's car seat. I refused to let him be mistreated ever again.

———

Currently, I was at the store grabbing a few things for DJ. He had outgrown the diapers I had at the house and he needed more milk.

He was asleep in his car seat in the cart.

As I walked down one of the aisles, I paused after spotting a familiar face. My mouth turned upwards as I made my way to her.

Reaching up, I grabbed the bottle Brenna was reaching for. "What you plan on making?" I handed it to her.

She turned to me with a shocked expression on her face. "Tae? Hey." Her mouth slowly formed into a smile. "What are you doing here?"

"Needed to grab a couple of things for him." I nodded towards the cart.

Brenna's eyes shifted to my cart. I held my breath, not really sure how she would respond to my son. I hadn't seen or talked to her since seeing her at *Mama's*, so I wasn't sure where her head was.

"He's so cute!" She gushed and leaned in, rubbing her fingers over his stomach lightly.

"Like daddy, like son." A crooked grin appeared on my face.

Brenna lifted her hand from DJ and faced me. Playfully she rolled her eyes.

"Whatever, ain't no one mention you." She tossed the sauce in her cart.

"You never answered my question. What are you making?"

Brenna stared at me with an expression I couldn't quite read before answering. "Chicken and steak Hibachi. I've been craving it but didn't want to order from anywhere."

My stomach rumbled at the thought. Brenna was a good cook when she wanted to be. There were a few times she threw down for me when we were seeing each other, and I was never disappointed.

"By the sound of your stomach, I take it that you're hungry?" She giggled and rose a brow.

"Hell, a nigga could eat." I rubbed my stomach.

Brenna brought her bottom lip between her teeth and shifted her eyes to my cart.

"If you don't have anything going on, you could follow me back to my house and get a plate."

Her words shocked me. I don't even remember the last time I was at Brenna's.

"My son-"

She gave me a small toothless smile. "Can come too, of course. No pressure though. Just know the offer stands." My heart skipped in my chest.

Brenna gave my son one last look. "I need to finish up my shopping."

Silently I stood there watching her as she walked off. The shorts she had on ate her ass, showing off the bottom of her cheeks. Even though she didn't have the fattest ass, it was still a nice view.

I didn't know if this was a genuine invitation or if Brenna was just being nice. The last thing I expected was for her to extend an invite to us.

"What you think, son? Should I take her up on her offer?" I looked down at DJ.

He was still asleep but shifted and brushed his balled up fist across his face causing me to laugh.

51

seven

Brenna

I WAS FINISHING up cooking while sipping on my LuxeMoné wine, bobbing my head to Summer Walker's first album that blared through Alexa.

"You know I love you like no one else could. I'd go to Hell and back for ya."

I chuckled at the lyrics as I checked on the veggies I planned on eating with my hibachi. The lyrics were a little out there, but I understood where she was coming from. Having such strong feelings for someone made you do things outside the norm.

I moved around my kitchen, getting a plate out of the cabinet and pouring myself some more wine while waiting for my food to finish cooking.

My mouth froze mid-sip when my doorbell went off. My brows furrowed together as my stomach flipped and my heart skipped a beat.

No one ever popped up at my house unannounced, so it could only be one person. Suddenly my hands grew sweaty and my pulse began to race.

When I extended the invite for Tae to come over, I halfway expected him to turn me down. I also surprised myself. If I was being honest, I missed being around him. It wasn't even on a sexual level. I missed his company. Devontae was a fixture in my life, always had been since Aisha and I became friends. Ignoring him and brushing him off wasn't easy because I was used to him.

My house wasn't large being that it was just me. It had three bedrooms, one of which I'd transformed into my office, and two baths. My kitchen and dining room were combined and across the walkway was my living room, giving me easy access to my front door.

With my wine glass still in hand, I inhaled a deep breath before opening the door. I wasn't even sure why I was nervous right now. Maybe it was because I hadn't been alone with Tae in months, or it could have been because his son was with him.

When I pulled open the door, I was stuck in a daze for a minute. I didn't give him much attention at the store, but now looking him over, I saw Tae was wearing the ultimate 'fuck boy' fit. Grey joggers gripped his thick, muscular thighs and showed off the print between his legs and he paired those with a black cut-off tee. His bulging arms were on full display, and his broad wide chest captured my attention. It looked like he had just stepped out of his barber's chair. His mustache was neatly lined up, and five o'clock shadow was in full effect.

Squeezing my thighs together, I smiled and stepped to the side.

"Hey. Come in."

Tae walked in with his son's car seat in hand and his diaper bag over his shoulder. This was the first time I would be alone with the two of them together, and that thought made me nervous all over again.

I closed the door behind them and turned to face him.

"You can have a seat in the living room." I walked past him and headed back to the kitchen.

I needed a moment to gather my thoughts. Once again, my impulsive nature caused me to act without thinking. When I saw

Tae at the store, a heat wave rushed through me and landed right between my legs. The yearning I felt for him had the words tumbling from my mouth before I could stop them.

"You need help with anything?" I jumped when Tae's deep baritone sounded right behind me. His hands went to my sides to steady me.

"My bad." He chuckled. "You lost in that big ass head and didn't hear me approach you."

Spinning around with my mouth turned up, I glared at him. "My head is not big!"

His hooded eyes peered into me. His hands were still on my waist and we were only centimeters apart.

My chest rose and fell quickly as I took him in again. "It's big as fuck, B." A crooked grin formed on his face.

Rolling my eyes, I pushed his solid chest, barely moving him. "Whatever, my head is cute."

Again, he chuckled. "It's a'right."

For a minute, we got lost in each other. Goosebumps ran up my arms. Suddenly the air in my kitchen was thick and hotter than normal.

Snatching my eyes from Tae's, I stepped back and turned back to the food. "I wasn't sure if you were coming so I didn't get you a plate. You can grab one out of the cabinet. Everything is ready."

"It smells good as fuck too!"

My chest warmed.

Silently I prepared me and Tae's food while he went to check on his son. Instead of eating at the dining room table, I brought the plates to the living room.

"Water to drink?"

He glanced up at me and nodded. "You know me so well."

Fighting back a smile, I grabbed him a bottled water from my fridge along with my wine glass.

Tae and I ate in a comfortable silence until halfway through when his son started whining.

"You mind if I use your room to change him?" Tae asked, taking DJ out of the car seat and grabbing his diaper bag.

My eyes focused on the baby. Seeing him side by side with his dad was a beautiful sight, honestly. It was like I was staring at Tae in baby form.

"Uh, no, you know where it is," I answered him.

"That I do." His words made the back of my neck heat up.

By the time Tae returned to the room, I had finished my food and placed my plate in the sink.

"This little nigga be smelling crazy," Tae spoke, walking through the kitchen to my back door. He unlocked it and pulled it open, stepping out onto my patio. Through the window above my sink, I watched him walk over to my garbage can and toss the dirty diaper inside.

I spun around when I heard DJ's small coos.

Slowly I made my way back to the living room and saw Tae had placed him in his car seat. He was smiling and babbling with wide eyes. I had been around him a few times when Aisha had him, and I wondered if he remembered me.

"You're a chunky little thing." I giggled, picking him up and sitting on my couch.

Drool ran down his mouth as he attempted to grab my face. "You're a messy fella too." I looked and saw a burping cloth in his car seat and grabbed it.

"He's teething right now." I heard from behind me.

Glancing over my shoulder, I saw Tae approaching us. "No wonder why." I wiped his mouth and tossed the cloth back in the car seat.

Tae took his seat next to me. "What are you feeding him?"

His eyes stayed trained on my face. I couldn't read the expression on his.

"All his ass do is eat and sleep. Greedy ass." He shook his head.

I snickered.

"I love chunky babies. Look at these cheeks." I pinched one of his cheeks, making him laugh.

"I thought kids weren't your thing."

I rolled my eyes. "Kids I can give back *are* my thing." I let him know, ignoring the dig at me.

Tae didn't reply. Instead, he picked his plate back up and continued eating.

"You threw down, B," he commented as he finished his food. "I can never call you a bad cook."

I still had DJ in my arms. He was now playing with the teething toy Tae had handed him.

"My mama wouldn't have it any other way." Tae walked to the kitchen with his plate.

This was foreign to me. Hanging out with a guy and his baby. I had never done this before. Although I had been around DJ before, it was never with his dad.

"Here, I can take him." Tae reached his arms out once he was back in the living room.

My nose scrunched up. "He's fine." I shooed his hands away.

He looked thrown off by my remark but didn't fight it.

"Thanks for inviting me over. All I been eating was meal preps for the past couple of weeks unless I went to my parents. It was nice having a real home cooked meal."

My shoulders rose then fell. "You know I always make too much anyways. It was no problem."

Once again, Tae stared at me with an expression I couldn't read. "This shit is crazy." He shook his head.

"What?"

His eyes darted from me to DJ. "You just casually holding my son, yet you stopped fucking with me because of him."

I opened my mouth to offer a rebuttal but snapped it shut just as quickly.

I wasn't entirely sure what to say to that. The conversation between Aisha and I flashed through my mind. It was hard learning the guy you were falling for was having a baby with someone who wasn't you. Not only that, although I knew he dealt with other women, I had convinced myself that I was the only one, which was stupid on my end. The bond I had with Tae made it easy to block everything else out.

"Tae," I spoke in a hushed breath, dropping my head.

"I'm just speaking facts."

When I lifted my head to face him again, I didn't see an upset expression on his face like I expected. In fact, he looked calm. His eyes raked over me.

"I'm sorry."

He lifted an eyebrow and pressed his lips together. "I made you feel like your son was an issue when in reality he wasn't."

When I glanced down, I noticed DJ was nodding off.

"Hand him here. His little ass gets heavier once he goes to sleep." This time I passed him DJ, who whined during the exchange.

I watched as Tae laid his son down in the car seat, then went into his diaper bag and grabbed the items to make him a bottle.

Seeing Tae like this wasn't new. He had basically been like a father to Bailey before Gage came into the picture. So, I'm not shocked by how good he was at this dad thing. It was different seeing him with *his kid* though. It was kind of sexy seeing him in daddy mode.

"Here you go, big fella." He propped the bottle under DJ's chin using the burping cloth. I snickered when his small chubby hands instantly wrapped around it. His eyes shot open for a moment before fluttering back closed.

"Greedy ass!" Tae shook his head.

"That's definitely your sister's nephew," I commented. One

thing about Aisha is she could eat. I'm surprised her ass was as little as she was.

"I know. He eats like a grown ass man. That's why I had to start adding cereal to his bottles. His doctor said it should help."

A small grin formed on my face. "You're good at this dad thing, huh?"

He slightly shrugged his shoulders as he put everything back in the diaper bag.

"I had practice with Bailey. She wasn't mine, but I felt like she was. It's different when it's your kid though. At the same time, I feel like I came into this situation with some insight."

Lazily I bobbed my head and glanced back down. DJ was still sucking on the bottle but had nodded off to sleep.

"He's so adorable. At least you made a cute kid."

"I mean, look at me. Did you expect anything less?"

"Ugh, you're so damn arrogant." I fake gagged while rolling my eyes.

"I got a reason to be. Don't you think?" His tongue swiped across his lips and he flexed his muscles.

My clit throbbed.

Blinking a couple of times, I focused on his face. "You ain't nothing to brag about."

A mischievous grin soon found its way onto his face. "Word?" He lifted a brow.

Before I could respond, Tae had grabbed me and yanked me over to his side. His lips found mine, immediately setting my body ablaze. Gripping his shirt tightly, I pushed my chest into his, melting against him.

Our tongues found each other, intertwining and wrestling fervently. An overwhelming tingle shot through my belly. My heart danced in excitement.

Suddenly Tae pulled away from me. Instantly my body felt cold.

"We need to finish our conversation." He nipped my bottom lip with his teeth. A low whimper escaped my mouth.

"What conversation?" My mind had gone blank as he dragged his lips over my jaw line, pressing them against it every so often.

"You said my son wasn't the reason you pulled away from me." My breath got caught in my throat as my eyes closed.

Tae rubbed on my bare thigh, sending heat to my center.

"He wasn't," I struggled to get out.

"Then what was it?" He had made his way to my neck. His hand crept closer to my yearning center. Without a second thought, I opened my legs wider, welcoming his touch.

"I, I." My words left me when he sucked roughly on my neck and brushed his fingers against my sex. I was still in my shorts, but my pussy knew he was close and grew wetter.

Tae pressed on my center, producing friction against my sensitive clit. My grip on his shirt grew tighter.

"You what?" Tae lifted up and my eyes fluttered open. His eyes were darker than normal. They were low and penetrating through me.

Swallowing hard, my mouth grew dry. "I was jealous," I admitted lowly. So low I wasn't sure if he could hear me.

Confusion filled his face. "Of what? My son?"

I shook my head quickly. I needed him to know my feelings didn't have anything to do with DJ, not directly at least.

Before I could explain what I meant, my doorbell went off.

The trance the two of us seemed to be in broke and our heads snapped to the door.

"Who's that?"

"I don't know." I pulled away from him and made my way to the door. My breathing returned to normal with each step I took away from Tae.

I checked the peephole and my stomach dropped when I

noticed Randy on the other side. I had completely forgotten about him.

"Shit," I muttered, looking over my shoulder. Tae was staring at me with a confused expression plastered on his face.

Pushing a heavy breath out, I unlocked my door and pulled it open.

"Randy?" I forced a smile on my face. "I wasn't expecting you back until next week."

He snatched me up in his arms and kissed me deeply. "I finished my meeting early and got an earlier flight."

The sincere happiness in his eyes as he gazed at me caused guilt to creep inside me.

"I, uh," I started but stopped. My words seemed to be at a loss.

"B, Ima holla at you later." I glanced over and saw Tae with DJ and his things preparing to leave.

When I brought my attention back to Randy, he looked perplexed. He released me slowly.

My stomach churched while my heart was pounding rapidly in my chest.

"Tae, I…it was good seeing you."

He turned to face me with a blank stare. Without replying, he gave me a crude nod and walked past us.

Randy was silent as I welcomed him into my house.

"Uh, want to sit?" I nodded to the couch. The moment I had just shared with Tae popped in my head, causing my cheeks to flush.

Randy's eyes seared into me, and his lips pressed tightly together. "Was I interrupting something?" he asked instead.

I wasn't sure what to say, so I slowly shook my head.

A sarcastic chuckle left his mouth. "Who was that?"

"Tae. Aisha's brother." Although he had never met Aisha before, he knew she was my best friend.

"And why was he here?"

"I cooked and invited him over for a plate."

A mocking smirk suddenly formed on his face. "And that's it?" A hint of amusement played in his voice.

Slowly my head moved up and down.

Randy licked his lips and shoved his hands in his pockets. "Don't bullshit me, Brenna." His voice was now low and gruff. It was a tone I had never heard from him before.

My face went blank. "What are you talking about?"

Randy swiped his thumb across his nose while giving me a stern look. "You fucking that nigga?"

My eyes bucked. "No," I instantly said.

It wasn't a complete lie. I hadn't had sex with Tae in over two months. Since the wedding.

"So, I guess that's a burn mark on your neck." Immediately my hand shot to my neck. My breathing slowed. I had no idea Tae was marking me as he kissed me. I shouldn't have been shocked though because he always said how sexy it was seeing his bite marks on me.

My eyes stayed trained on Randy. I knew it was no sense in lying now. Plus, he didn't deserve it. He was a good dude, just not for me.

"I'm not fucking him…anymore." My hand slowly left my neck and hooked on my wrist in front of me. "Tae and I used to deal with each other, but we stopped right before I met you. I thought I was over him. I tried to get over him, but…." My words trailed off as my shoulder lifted.

Tonight showed that Tae wasn't out of my system like I had hoped. It wouldn't be fair to Randy or myself to keep acting as if I was over him.

"I knew some shit wasn't right with you." My face balled up. I went to speak, but he continued.

"I felt like you were holding back. Like something was up. I didn't think you were dealing with someone else, but I knew it was something."

"I'm sorry, Randy. You're a great guy, and I-"

"You're right, I am." He cut me off, causing my mouth to turn upside down. "All you had to do was be straight up with me, and I would have understood."

I bobbed my head. "You're going to make some lucky woman happy one day."

This time his face softened. "Too bad it's not you. You take care of yourself, Brenna."

Silently I watched him turn and make his exit. I felt bad about how things had gone down, but at the same time, I couldn't keep lying to myself.

Once Randy was gone and I was alone, I couldn't help but exhale a large breath. I had turned off Alexa once we started eating, and now my house was wryly quiet.

I turned and looked around my space.

Part of me wanted to call Tae back over. I already missed his presence, but I refrained.

Tonight had been a lot, and by the look on his face when he left, I knew I wasn't his favorite person right now.

Sighing, I gripped the back of my neck.

Tonight didn't go as planned, but I was happy that I was able to end things with Randy and figure my feelings for Tae out.

eight

Devontae

"YOUR CASE LOOKS STRONG. I believe you have a good chance of winning," Diya spoke as she glanced at me over her notepad.

She finally got back to me, and we were able to schedule a meeting. I had been here for over an hour going over my case. Thankfully, Tia posted everything on social media, so I was able to show her proof of my concerns. I also had the pictures from when I picked my son up from her home and the proof of lack of communication on her behalf.

"Man, I'm glad to hear that." I bit down on my bottom lip.

Diya stared at me sincerely. "I'm going to be honest with you. Most of the time, courts favor the mother in custody battles, but from what you've told and shown me, you have a pretty solid case. I'll get everything together and file the paperwork in the morning."

I nodded my head. "Is there anything else I need to do?"

"Just keep a record of everything you provide for your son. Keep a record of all of Tia's actions. This could get ugly. Don't let her provoke you in any way. I've seen custody battles bring out the worst in people."

"You don't have to worry about that. I don't have shit to say to her."

"Good." Diya stood up, prompting me to do the same. "I look forward to working with you." She held her hand out.

I shook it and thanked her before turning to leave her office.

Once I stepped outside and the sun hit my skin, I felt like a weight had been lifted from my shoulders. Hopefully, Tia wouldn't put up too much of a fight regarding giving me custody. It was obvious she had no desire to be a mother.

My phone vibrated as I made my way to my car.

Reaching in my pocket, I took it out and unlocked it.

> **Baby sis:** *Can you bring ice when you come? I think we're going to need more than what we have.*
> **Me:** *I gotchu.*

Gage and Aisha were throwing one last gathering at their house before the basketball season started.

I found Kaia's name and sent her a text letting her know I was on my way and to have DJ dressed. So far, she's turned out to be a blessing. My schedule was more structured, but my days could be long, especially when I did in-house training. She never complained, and DJ seemed to love her.

Things finally seemed like they were looking up.

———

"Aht aht, who told you to come over here in some hoochie daddy shorts!" My sister's voice sounded behind me.

Whipping around, I chuckled. "What the fuck are hoochie daddy shorts, Aisha?"

"You know! The ones you're wearing, the ones that go mid-thigh showing off all the goods." She balled her face up. "Don't nobody wanna see that."

I glanced down at my shorts and then back at her. "Man, get out of here." I chuckled. "Where do you want this ice?"

"Give me my baby. The coolers are over by the tables." She reached for DJ, and he happily went to her.

"Where's your two?" I asked, looking around.

"Bailey is in the pool, and Brenna has Brooklyn."

A sharp pain pierced my chest at the mention of Brenna. I hadn't spoken to her since leaving her house, not that she hadn't reached out. I just wasn't feeling her.

Seeing her kiss and hug up on the nigga that showed up at her door caused jealousy to shoot through me, and it took everything in me to just walk away. I thought me and Brenna were coming to an understanding that night.

It felt good having her back in my arms. The way her body melted into mine felt like we were getting back on track. Since we started dealing with each other, I hadn't seen her with another guy. I knew she dated but seeing it in my face didn't feel good.

I wasn't afraid to admit I was a possessive nigga. When something was mine, I didn't like to share.

Walking over to the coolers, I opened them along with the ice and filled the one that needed more.

Standing up, I looked around the yard and saw my dad and Gage's dad on the grill. Our moms were off to the side, gossiping more than likely.

A few of Gage's teammates were in attendance, along with Elijah.

I located Brenna sitting at one of the tables with Brooklyn in her arms.

"Uncle Tae!" My attention dropped as Bailey came rushing up to me.

"Wassup, Bai Bai!" I would have hugged her, but she was soaked from being in the pool.

She wiped some hair that was sticking to her face out the way. "Where's my cousin!"

I turned my mouth upside down. "You don't want to kick it with me?"

She giggled and shook her head. "Damn, that's messed up, Bai." I grabbed my heart like I was hurt, only making her laughs grow louder. "Your mom has *your cousin.*"

Bailey didn't waste any time turning and sprinting off in search of her cousin.

Turning back to the cooler, I picked a beer up and cracked it open.

"When did you get here?" I glanced over and saw Gage approaching me.

"A few minutes ago." I stood and brought the beer to my mouth.

"How did meeting with the lawyer go?"

Crossing my arms over my chest, I scanned the yard again. Of course, my eyes landed back on Brenna. Aisha was now sitting next to her with Bailey on her side and my son in her lap. My heart stuttered in my chest. As much as I wanted to walk over there, I refrained. Brenna had a nigga, and I wasn't the one to play second.

"Good. She told me she thinks I have a strong case."

"That's what up. I know you didn't want to do this, but it'll be good in the long run."

I nodded. "I know. It's just fucked up that it has to come to this."

For a second, the two of us grew quiet. "It's crazy because two years ago you weren't even sure if you wanted to be a father and now look at yo ass." I brought my beer bottle to my mouth.

Gage laughed. "I know, shits wild. Now I can't picture myself not being a parent. I'm glad Aisha didn't give up on me."

"I still can't believe you were sleeping with my little sister all that damn time. I had no clue."

Gage's laugh grew louder. "We was slick as fuck with that shit, huh?"

I mugged him. "Y'all lucky I didn't find out then because I would have nipped that shit in the bud."

Gage waved me off. "How you talking shit but you fucking yo sister's best friend?"

My eyes locked on Brenna. She had her head tossed back, laughing at something my sister had said. I always loved how chinky her eyes grew when she laughed.

"That's different."

Gage crossed his arms. "How?"

My tongue dragged across my lips and I stayed quiet. In reality, it wasn't different, but I wasn't going to admit that shit.

"Exactly! The only difference was I was fucking with your sister since high school." Again, I mugged him.

"What y'all niggas over here talking about?" Elijah walked up and slapped hands with me.

"About how I been fucking on Aisha for years."

The two of them laughed while my face dropped. "Keep on and I'ma rock yo shit." Gage waved me off.

"Anyways, c'mon, let's get a dominos or spades game started. I'm feeling lucky today." Elijah rubbed his hands together.

"I'm game." I took a sip of my beer and headed over.

"Let me go check on the food and I'll meet y'all under the tent.

On my way to the tent, I stopped and spoke to both my and Gage's mom. My mom's first question was where my son was, and once I let her know Aisha had him, she walked off to grab him. It was wild how irrelevant you became once you had a kid.

"Devonte." I heard behind me.

Turning around, I noticed my dad. He nodded his head for me to come to him.

"Wassup Pops." I took a drink of my beer.

"How did things go with Diya?"

"Good. She thinks we can win with ease." He bobbed his head.

"Good. She's a shark in the courtroom. You can put your faith in her."

"How do you know her again?" I side eyed him.

"I worked with her dad for years. He never failed to brag about how good of an attorney she was."

I nodded.

My dad slapped my shoulder and cuffed it. "You'll be a full-time single father. You ready for that?"

My attention went to my son, who was now in my mom's arms. He was laughing and being his normal happy self.

"I am. There isn't anything I wouldn't do for him."

"I wouldn't expect anything less."

I stood there talking to my dad for a little longer before my name was called. It looked like the guys were all set up for the game.

"Go ahead." My dad stepped back.

I made my way to the tent. On my way there my eyes found their way back to Brenna. This time we locked eyes. She gave me a small smile that I didn't return. Taking my attention away from her, I continued toward the tent.

I had no words for Brenna or time for whatever game she was trying to play.

nine

Brenna

MY HEART SQUEEZED when Tae turned away from me with an emotionless expression on his face. It was obvious he was still holding on to what happened at my house. If only he had given me a chance to explain, he would know I ended things with Randy.

Rolling my eyes, I turned my focus back to Aisha, who was smirking at me while feeding Brooklyn.

"What?"

"You and my brother still haven't made up, huh?"

"Your brother is a major pain in my ass," I scoffed.

Aisha snickered. "That's what your mouth is saying, but your face says something different." My nose bunched up.

"What's that supposed to mean?"

"You're not over him." She shrugged and removed the baby from under the blanket and covered herself back up. It still amazed me that she was so comfortable just whipping her boob out to feed Brooklyn. I mean, this was her house and everything, but still. She placed the same blanket on her shoulder and tapped Brooklyn's back.

"Why don't you just go talk to him? Isn't that what you used to tell me about Gage?" My head tilted to the side.

I glanced back at the tent Tae had disappeared into, seeing the guys crowded around a table.

"Nah, I'm good." I wasn't about to embarrass myself in front of all those people. If Tae wanted to be upset about a misunderstanding, then that was his business.

Aisha smacked her lips. "You ended things with Randy, right?"

I nodded my head. "Okay, and you said him having a kid isn't an issue, right?"

Again, I nodded. "So, what's stopping you from making up with him?"

My brows dipped together and I twisted my mouth to the side. "Why are you pushing this so hard?"

"Because both you and my brother look miserable. Also, it's awkward as hell when we're all together and the two of you refuse to acknowledge each other. Instead, you just steal glances at each other. Y'all need to fix y'all shit so we can all move on."

Brooklyn burped, and when Aisha pulled her away, I noticed she had fallen asleep. "I'm going to lay my baby down." She stood up.

I sighed and leaned back in my chair, bringing the bottle of sweet tea to my mouth. I knew I wasn't trying to continue this back and forth with Tae, but I wasn't sure if he would hear me out either. He looked pretty pissed off when he left my house.

Instead of dwelling on the situation, I attempted to push it to the back of my mind.

"TT, swim with me!" Bailey rushed over to me and begged. Bailey was the cutest little kid. She had so much life inside her that her spirit always spilled into whoever she was around.

I smiled at my oldest Godchild. "If you insist." I finished the rest of my tea and stood up.

Following Bailey, I walked over to Gage's newly renovated

in-ground pool, pushed down the shorts I had on, and pulled my tank top off, tossing both to the side.

Bailey cannonballed into the pool, and I dove in headfirst.

The water was the perfect temperature. Although it was cold, the sun had made it bearable.

"TT!" Bailey splashed me.

I cut my eyes at her. "I'ma get you!" I swam over to her.

She laughed and tried to get away. It was a good thing her mom put her in swimming lessons.

"Damn, y'all just forgot about me!" Aisha called out from the deck.

"C'mon, mommy!" Bailey laughed.

I reached her and instantly started tickling her.

Aisha stripped down to her bathing suit and started towards the stairs that led into the pool. "Okay, baddie!" I called out.

Brooklyn had thickened her frame. Although she still held a little baby weight in her mid-section, everything else looked good.

"I know Brooklyn did the body good!" She laughed.

We stayed in the pool for a while until she and Gage's dad announced the food was ready.

I stayed back and let everyone go and wash their hands so they could grab a plate. I kept my clothes off but had a towel wrapped around me.

Once the coast was clear, I walked into the house and went to the bathroom on the first floor. After emptying my bladder, I washed my hands and prepared to leave the bathroom.

"Shit!" I yelped when I opened the door and saw Tae on the other side. The serious expression on his face made my stomach quake.

Without my permission, my eyes took him in. The hoochie daddy shorts he had on gave a full display of his perfectly toned, muscular thighs. Obviously, he took leg day seriously.

"Excuse me." I attempted to walk past him, but it was like

trying to get past a brick wall. "Excuse you!" I shrieked when he pushed me back into the bathroom. He shut the door behind him and locked it all while keeping his hard glare on me.

I swallowed hard, feeling anxious about how this could go.

"I'm trying to go eat," I let him know.

His eyes cut into tight slits. "That was your nigga who showed up at your crib?" His arms crossed over his chest. I shamelessly ogled his swollen arms as they flexed. He was in a wife beater and small beads of sweat were on his top half.

Memories of how he would easily swoop me up and fuck me in the air filled my mind. I pushed a deep breath out.

"No. It was someone I was dealing with, but I ended things." His dark orbs raked over my body. I had lost the towel since entering the bathroom, leaving me in the yellow two-piece.

A spark of some indefinable emotion flashed through his eyes when he found my face again. His jaw slightly flexed before pressing into a straight line.

My skin prickled with goosebumps.

I was trying to read what was going on in his head, but his expression was a mask of stone.

"Tae," I spoke lowly.

My heart rate skyrocketed.

Even though he was wearing a serious expression, I couldn't deny that my center throbbed for him.

I wanted him to touch me. I wanted to touch him.

The desire building inside me for this man was shameful, honestly, but I didn't care at this moment.

As if Tae could read my mind and sense my urges, he rushed me before I could blink.

His hand went to my neck and he forced me back against the sink. His mouth found mine and he kissed me savagely.

His large hands went to my breasts.

Flashes of him fucking me at Aisha's wedding replayed in my mind.

It was like a raging river between my legs as he groped and kissed me. None of his gestures were soft and sweet, but I liked them.

"You keep fucking playing with me like I'm some sucka ass nigga."

I yelped when his teeth sunk into my neck.

My eyes rolled to the back of my head when his hand found its way into my bikini bottoms. He rubbed on my lower lips, teasing and pitching my clit every so often.

Gripping his strong arms, I sunk my nails into them. Thankfully, I was against the sink because my knees buckled the moment he inserted his fingers in me.

One, then two.

He pumped them in and out of me. My hips moved against them, desperately chasing the orgasm I knew only he could bring me.

Tae's lips came back to mine, capturing them hungrily.

My pussy locked around his fingers.

His fingers pinched my nipples and a small whimper escaped my mouth.

My eyes squeezed shut.

Just as I felt myself about to cum, Tae snatched his hand from between my legs. My eyes popped open and I glared at him.

"Why would you do that!" I squealed.

His eyes darkened and narrowed.

"You don't deserve to cum yet."

Tae snatched me up and sat me on the sink.

I was about to speak again when he pushed down his shorts and briefs, shutting me up instantly.

My pussy leaked more at the sight of the beauty that hung between his legs. Tae's dick honestly deserved an award. It was beautiful. It was the same golden color as his skin, thick, veiny, and long with a slight hook to the left at the tip.

Tae stroked himself while staring at me as if I was his prey.

Slowly he made his way to me. Grabbing my thighs, he pulled me to the edge of the sink. I lined up perfectly with his shaft.

His hand went back to my neck and he gripped it. My eyes rolled to the back of my head.

While crashing his mouth down to mine, he lined his member up with my awaiting sex and pushed into me roughly.

A low grunt left my mouth, falling into his.

Tae fucked me roughly on the sink, keeping his hand on my neck.

With his other hand, he snatched down my bikini top and groped my breast.

My hands went to the sink, gripping it tightly, taking the pleasurable punishment he was giving me.

"Tell me this my pussy, B," he grunted into my mouth, biting down on my bottom lip.

I attempted to speak, but the way he was fucking me snatched both my words and breath away.

His grip on my neck was tight. "I said, tell me this my pussy." His mouth left mine and dropped down to my breast. He flicked his tongue over my pebbled nipple before pulling it to his mouth.

His strokes went deeper and were stronger than before.

"Tae!" I whined as my stomach tightened.

Squeezing my eyes shut, I tried to hold off the orgasm building inside me.

"Tell me what I want to hear." The change in his voice and stroke caused me to open my eyes and stare into his.

The passion and fire smoldering through them caused my chest to tighten.

"Tell me it's mine." His mouth was now centimeters from mine. His smokey tone caused my body to tremble.

"It's yours," I admitted in a strained voice.

A cocky grin formed on his face. "That a girl."

He pumped in and out of me with steady strokes, tapping my spot repeatedly until I was raining on his dick.

"Can I cum in you?" he asked throatily. "Can I claim my pussy?"

Tremors shot through my chest as he kissed me slowly and passionately.

"Yes!" I cried, gripping the sink so tight that I'm sure my knuckles were white.

His hand moved from my neck and went to my side. His fingers sunk into my flesh. His dick massaged my walls, the tip of it knocked against my spot. As if it was tapping on a button, my walls released and I was cumming again.

Tae's fingers sunk deeper into my side, and I felt his dick jump inside me before he shot his seeds deep inside me.

"Fuckkk!" he growled, dropping his head to my neck.

His teeth sunk into my shoulder and it caused me to cum harder.

Both of our breathing was choppy and sweat dripped from our bodies.

I lowered my head on Tae's and closed my eyes, attempting to regulate my breathing.

After a few minutes of silence, Tae was pulling out of me. A small moan escaped my lips.

I watched as Tae reached around me and ripped some paper towels off the roll. He reached behind me to wet them then placed them between my lips.

I winced, feeling some soreness.

Tae glanced at me with a smirk on his face.

Rolling my eyes, I pushed him away and hopped down.

I fixed my top, and as I bent down to grab my bottoms, he came up behind me, pressing himself against my ass.

When I stood up, he wrapped his arms around my waist and pulled me into his chest.

"You know we need to have a real conversation, right?" He pulled the top of my ear into his mouth then sucked on it.

"I know," I whispered as my breathing slowed.

Tae kissed my ear a few more times before making his way down to my neck.

He spun me around so that I was facing him. A hardened expression was on his face.

He must have talked himself out of whatever he was about to say. Instead, he shook his head, pecked my lips, and stepped back.

"Go ahead and get yourself together."

"You're not gone wipe yourself off?" I noticed he now had those damn shorts back on. His dick sat proudly in the front of them.

"Nah." One corner of his mouth rose in a smirk. "I like the thought of *us* lingering on me."

A chill shot through my body.

Tae left me in the bathroom.

The moment I was alone, I leaned against the sink with my hand on my chest. My heart was still pounding wildly in my chest, slamming against my ribcage.

It amazed me every time Tae touched me my body went into a frenzy as if it was the first time. The connection I had with that man was undeniable, and I knew there was no sense in denying it any longer.

———

"Don't try to sneak out here like you and brother wasn't being nasty in my house! I hope you cleaned up after your-selves." I jumped and dropped the cheeseburger in my hand on my plate.

"Shit!" I gasped.

Aisha laughed and took a seat next to me.

I had snuck out of the house unnoticed, or so I thought, and made a plate. Finding a spot away from everyone, I tried gathering myself. After what just happened in the bathroom, all I wanted to do was curl up in bed and go to sleep.

"Shouldn't you be somewhere with your husband?" I cut my eyes at her then picked my burger back up.

"He's too into his card game to notice me right now." She waved me off.

Biting into my burger, I closed my eyes, savoring the taste. Whoever seasoned them did their thing.

"Are you and my brother good now?"

"Aisha, what are you talking about?" I swallowed and looked at her.

"Don't play with me. Y'all both disappeared for a good twenty minutes. Then he came out of the house smiling. Your ass is glowing. I can put two and two together." She scrunched her face up. "I really hope y'all cleaned up after yourselves."

I sniffled a snicker. "Everything is clean, Aisha."

I bit into the burger again.

Her eyes drilled into the side of my face. "And I hope y'all ain't wake my baby up."

I snorted. "The baby is still sleeping."

Satisfied with my answers, she let up.

"So are y'all good?"

My shoulders rose then fell. Lifting my face, my eyes found Tae. His son was now in his hands while he spoke to one of Gage's teammates.

Tae said we needed to talk, and I agreed. We needed to hash out a lot of gray areas between us.

"Aisha," Gage's deep baritone called out.

Aisha's face instantly lit up and she popped up.

"Why do I feel like I haven't seen yo ass all day?" He pulled her into him and kissed her.

Aisha giggled and wrapped her arms around his neck. The

love they shared was beautiful. Knowing their story and how they overcame all the obstacles between them showed me that maybe Tae and I could make whatever this was work.

When I looked back at him, his eyes were already trained on me. He winked and gave me a crooked grin.

Heat rushed to my cheeks.

I pushed back the thoughts of us leaving and finishing what we started in the bathroom. We had to hurry and figure our shit out. This aimless dancing we kept doing was starting to take a toll on me.

———

"You just gone stand there or come inside?" Tae asked me, holding his door open.

We were leaving Gage and Aisha's house when he stopped me and told me to follow him to his house. I guess when he said we needed to talk, he meant now.

"Shut up." I cut my eyes at him and walked into the house.

He chortled lowly, shutting the door behind me.

Making my way out of his foyer to his living room, I waited for him to join me.

"Where's DJ?" I asked, looking around. A few baby items were scattered on the floor.

Tae's house used to look like a straight bachelor pad, down to the black and grey interior. Now there were baby things all around it.

"He's sleeping in his room."

Tae sat next to me, turning his body to face me.

"You wanted me to follow you, so obviously, you had something on your mind," I stated.

Tae gave me a once over. I was back in my clothes, but by the way he was staring at me, you would think I was still in my bathing suit or naked.

"We need to come to an understanding."

I bobbed my head in agreeance. "I agree." I swallowed hard. "I want to be with you," I stated simply.

No more would I fight my feelings for him. It had been a long couple of months without him, and as much as I tried to act unaffected, I wasn't. I missed Tae, everything about him I craved daily.

"Who was that nigga that popped up at yo house?" he asked with his top lip curled.

"Someone I used to deal with, but I ended things." I kept it simple.

"When?"

"That same night."

His jaw flexed. "Why?"

My eyes dropped to where his hands were resting on his thighs. "Because I knew nothing would come of us because I was still stuck on you."

Lifting my eyes back to his face, I watched his reaction to my words.

"I filed for full custody of my son." His statement caught me off guard. I blinked a few times while he continued.

"I'm about to be a full-time single father. The next person I deal with has to be able to accept that. As much as I would like to say I'll always be available, I can't promise that. He's going to demand a lot of my time. I know that was an issue for you before."

I nibbled on the corner of my bottom lip and thought about my next words. Yes, I would love to be the one who got all of Tae's time. We used to have some fun and spirited times together. It was part of the reason I enjoyed being with him.

"Your sister helped me realize that my main problem was I was jealous that another woman had your baby. Even though we never stated that we were exclusive, I guess in my head, I had come to the conclusion that we were. I at least thought you weren't just having sex with anyone but me unprotected. I don't know. I guess I just felt as if what we had was special."

I tugged on my bottom lip with my teeth and looked at everything but him. It wasn't easy for me to be open with my feelings, but I knew if I wanted a relationship with Tae, I needed to put everything on the table.

When his hand landed on my thigh, my focus went back on him. This time his face was softer.

"First, I wasn't fucking Tia raw. The condom broke, and instead of me making sure she took the Plan B, I just trusted she would. Her getting pregnant wasn't planned or wanted, although I love my son. And if it makes you feel any better, I was just fucking you. I fucked Tia after Aisha had caught us and we stopped talking for that little minute."

I didn't know how much I needed to hear that until the words left his mouth. It brought a sense of comfort to me.

"I'm selfish and needy, Tae," I explained.

"You telling me that shit like I don't know that already."

"I'm not always good with expressing how I feel."

He gave me another 'tell me something I don't know' look.

"But I can't help but want you. I know your son is a package deal, and I'm willing to try if you're willing."

My fingers tapped on the sides of my legs as I awaited his answer.

"I have faith in you, B. I've seen you interact with my son, and I have no doubt we can make this work."

"And your baby mama?"

"Won't be an issue. She ain't shit to me."

Feeling my heart swell, I scurried closer to Tae and grabbed his face, pressing my lips against his.

My head spun as our kiss grew deeper.

I was going to put my doubts and worries aside and put faith in what I felt. I was always an impulsive person, but it's time for me to use that on my heart.

ten

Devontae

WHILE TAKING a break from my workout, I received a text from Brenna. The moment I opened it, I almost choked on my water while laughing.

> **B:** *Screenshot attached* DELETE THIS NOW!

Smirking, I quickly replied.

> **Me:** *Why? I gotta promote my services.*

It didn't take long for her to respond. When I read it over, it only made me laugh harder.

> **B:** *Your dick is on full display! DELETE & TRY AGAIN!*

Chuckling, I pulled up my InstaFlik and went to the picture she was complaining about. The post was letting my followers know I was accepting new clients. It was a shirtless picture of me before I started my workout. Brenna was trippin' because the shorts I wore showed the outline of my dick, but I couldn't help I blessed in that area. I didn't know what the fuck she expected me to do.

Clicking on the post, I snorted at the comments. There were a lot of thirsty ass females, claiming they would come work out only if I were going to be their trainer.

Exiting the app, I was about to respond to Brenna when a call came through.

Instantly I felt my temples begin to throb and my blood boil.

Rolling my neck between my shoulders, my brows pinched together as I hit the green button.

"Finally calling to ask about your son?" I spoke flatly.

"*Custody*!" Tia bellowed in my AirPods. I quickly turned the volume down. "You're suing me for full custody of my son?"

Not bothering to get worked up, I reminded myself to stay calm. I wanted to curse her ass out, being that it had been two weeks since I picked my son up from her, yet this was the first time I was hearing from her.

"I'm suing for custody of *my son,* yes. You don't give a fuck about him, Tia, and I'm not going to make him suffer because of that." I tried to keep my voice steady, but it was hard. "You haven't even called to check on him.

Tia scoffed. "Check on him for what! You're his father!"

Chewing on the inside of my jaw, I shook my head. The pounding in my head increased.

"You know how fucking stupid you sound? Regardless of if I'm his father or not, *you're his mother* and should still call to check on him. My son will be better off with me, and I'ma make sure that happens. Not get the fuck off my line."

She started yelling something else, but I hung up in the middle of it.

Tia was the least of my concerns. Our first court date was scheduled for the end of the month, and I was hoping I would get temporary custody until the final ruling.

Locking my phone, I slide it back into my armband.

Speaking with Tia had ruined my mood, and the urge to push myself in my workout consumed me.

My music started playing as I made my way to the weights.

———

"Okay, DJ, show daddy what we've been working on!" Kaia boasted, sitting DJ on all fours and moving backward.

I stood in front of them with a smile on my face and arms crossed, watching intently. The past couple of days, I have been keeping DJ close. Hearing from his mom the other day stirred a strong sense of protection in me. She was pissed; I wasn't sure why because she didn't give a damn about my son.

Today I had two clients back-to-back and had just got home. One of the many things I appreciated about Kaia was that she worked with DJ regarding his development and learning. Her educational background was a big plus.

DJ laughed and babbled as he rocked.

My eyes widened thinking he was about to crawl until he fell back on his ass and started mimicking Kaia by clapping his hands.

"Damn, son." I chuckled.

"We're still working on it, but he's got the rocking part down, which is good."

I smiled at Kaia. "You've been a lifesaver. I really appreciate all you do for him." Because my family felt some kind of way, I only had her here 2-3 times a week unless something came up out of the blue. Any other time I took DJ to my parents' house. Aisha had returned to work, and although she said I could drop DJ off at the shop anytime, I chose not to.

Kaia's face lit up. "I love DJ! He's such a sweet and loving baby. We have a great time together, don't we!" She moved over and tickled his belly.

My smile grew until someone started knocking on my door like a madman.

"Who the fuck," I muttered and turned to go to my foyer.

Pulling my phone out, I accessed my cameras and clicked on the outside one.

Seeing the person on the other side, I hurriedly opened the door.

"Brenna? What are you doing here and in the rain?" I questioned. The dress she was wearing was soaked and hugging her body.

She swiped the rain off her face and bounced on the balls on her feet. "I have to pee really bad and your house was closer than mine! Please move!"

She pushed past me before I could respond to her. I watched as she rushed to my bedroom, which was on the first floor. It held the closest bathroom. The half bath was on the other side of the house next to the kitchen, and the other full bath was upstairs.

I walked through the foyer back to the living room.

"Is everything okay?" Kaia asked, bouncing DJ on her lap. He was now seven months, and the older he got, the more active he became.

"Yeah, everything's good." I nodded and glanced over my shoulder towards my room. "Oh, I forgot to ask, are you able to come Saturday morning instead of the afternoon? The guy I'm training needed to swap times."

Kaia nodded. "That shouldn't be a problem."

"Great. My session starts at 10."

"Hey, I hope you don't mind, but I grabbed a towel to-" Brenna's words drifted off.

I turned to face her and noticed she was frowning at Kaia and DJ. "Oh, I didn't realize you had company." Her voice went flat.

I could see the assumptions bouncing around in her head. Her face fell just as flat as her voice was.

Brenna narrowed her eyes and cut them in my direction.

Kaia must have sensed Brenna's instant mood change. "Uhm, I should head out, Tae. I'll see you Saturday." She stood up and wiped her hands over the joggers she was wearing.

"I know you fucking lying," Brenna mumbled. My eyes briefly went to her.

Giving her a small smile, I nodded. "It's about time for DJ's nap. You mind putting him down before you go?"

Her eyes bounced from Brenna and back to me before giving me a simple nod. "Of course."

"Thank, Kaia." I smiled at her.

Turning around to face Brenna, I noted how she was shooting daggers at Kaia. I'm sure if looks could kill, I would be in search of a new babysitter.

"C'mere." I didn't give her time to protest.

Grabbing her arm, I pulled her in the direction of my bedroom. She didn't put up a fight, thankfully.

The moment we were in my room, Brenna snatched away and started ranting.

"If we were still sleeping with other people, you could have said that, Tae!"

I stayed close to the door and crossed my arms over my chest as I leaned on it.

"What are you talking about, B?" My head cocked to the side. I kept my voice leveled.

"You and whoever that girl is! Don't act like I didn't just walk in on-"

Pushing myself off the door, I took two big steps towards her until I was in her face. I could tell my sudden movement caught her off guard because she stumbled back with wide eyes.

"Walk in on what? What did you walk in on, Brenna?" I stepped closer to her and glared down at her.

She swallowed hard and narrowed her eyes. Her hands went

to my chest as if she were about to push me back. I grabbed her small wrist.

"Like I didn't walk in on you and her being all cozy with DJ. And why would she see you Saturday? What y'all got a date?"

The jealousy pouring out of Brenna was cute and was causing my dick to rise. I smirked and it only made her scowl deepen.

I yanked her into me. "I don't think I've ever seen you this jealous before, B." A hint of amusement played in my voice.

She scoffed. "Jealous? I'm not jealous. I just think it's disrespectful that you have some girl in your house after we agreed to give this relationship a shot and-"

"She's DJ's babysitter," I cut her off.

Brenna's mouth snapped shut. Her eyes searched mine. "What?"

I licked my lips and tightened my hold on her wrist. "She's the babysitter. I'm not fucking that girl, never fucked that girl, and don't plan on fucking that girl."

Brenna's cheeks grew red and her eyes shifted to the side. "Oh." I chuckled.

"Yeah, oh." Letting go of her hand, I grabbed her chin, forcing her to maintain eye contact. I stared at her for a moment without speaking, taking her beauty in. Her hair was starting to curl up from the rain.

"Did I ever tell you how much I like this short look on you?"

Brenna slowly shook her head. "Well, I do. It's sexy as hell."

She opened her mouth but closed it right away.

"You don't have shit to say now, huh?"

Her eyes squinted. "You never mentioned having a young babysitter. How was I supposed to know?"

"For one, you could have asked." She rolled her eyes.

A small chortle fell from my lips.

"We need to get you out of these wet clothes."

"I should head home then."

I shook my head, tucking my bottom lip between my teeth.

Stepping closer, I forced her to step back until she was at my king-size bed.

"Nah, that's not what I had in mind."

Lowering my head, I captured her lips with mine. My hands went to her hips and slid down until they gripped her thighs.

Bending down, I lifted her up, and she instantly wrapped her legs around my waist. She hugged my neck and connected her lips with my mine.

Spinning around, I sat on my bed with her straddling me.

Brenna grinded against my hard dick. It was painfully hard, begging to be released.

Reaching between us, I removed my dick from my basketball shorts. My hands slipped under her dress and I gripped her ass, jiggling it.

"Mhm, your ass got bigger." I bit on her bottom lip.

"Happy weight."

"Nah, that's good dick weight."

Brenna pulled up and stared at me lustfully.

She reached down and moved her panties to the side before finding my shaft and lowering herself on it.

Her mouth dropped and eyes fluttered as I filled her.

Brenna's pussy hugged my pole and coated it with her juices. She started slowly rolling her hips on top of me but little did she know, this wasn't this kind of party.

One corner of my mouth rose.

I spread her ass cheeks and lifted her then slammed her down on me.

She moaned loudly and stared at me with wide eyes.

"You got me fucked up coming in here yelling and shit," I gritted as I continued slamming her down on me. Her legs unwrapped from around me and fell to the side.

"I didn't," she cried as I thrust upwards.

Ignoring her, I stood up and turned to lay her down on the

bed. My hands went behind her knees. I lifted her legs in the air, holding them and pumping in and out of her. Each time I pushed into her, her body jerked and her moans grew louder.

Her hold on my dick grew tighter and her back arched.

"Pull your dress down," I demanded. It was a halter top.

Doing as I requested, Brenna grabbed the front of her dress and yanked it down. My dick grew harder, watching her breasts freely bounce as I fucked her.

She grabbed her breasts and squeezed them, tossing her head back and closing her eyes.

"Fuck, you're so fucking sexy!" I pushed her legs back further so I could sink deeper inside her.

"Tae, you're too deep!" she cried.

"I'm not deep enough." Her walls grew tighter around me and her tunnel became even wetter.

My eyes dropped down. My dick was drowning in her juices.

Brenna's body jerked and she released a loud moan as she came.

Before she could fully finish, I snatched out of her and dropped down, covering her pussy with my mouth. Her body jerked as I licked and sucked on her clit, pulling the hood back to give me better access.

"Shit!" Her hand went to my head.

My eyes shot up, and I watched as she massaged her breasts while pushing my head further into her sex.

I happily devoured her lower lips. Pushing two fingers inside her and fucking her with them.

When she got louder and her body trembled, I swiped my tongue across her wet slit and pulled back.

Her eyes shot open and she glared at me. Ignoring her, I stood up and held her legs in the crook of my arms, pushing my way back into her.

Her face twisted.

"I'm about to fill this pussy, B," I groaned, rolling my hips into her.

"Fill it," she cried, rubbing on her clit.

The sight was sexy as hell.

I stroked her with steady strokes, rotating between fast and slow.

Brenna's body arched and her eyes rolled to the back of her head.

As soon as her pussy constricted around me, I was letting off inside of her.

My body jerked and my eyes squeezed shut.

Dropping her legs, I leaned over and kissed her hungrily. My hands pushed hers out the way and fondled her breasts. My dick was still leaking inside of her.

Brenna hugged my neck tightly.

Our wet bodies pressed against each other.

My heart swelled in my chest and blood rushed through my veins.

"Fuck, I love you," I mumbled against her mouth.

Her eyes expanded and she stared at me in a daze.

"I love you too."

"Don't doubt me again." I pecked her lips.

Brenna nodded and pulled my face closer to hers.

———

"What are we doing here?" Brenna asked once I put my car in park. She looked over at me with a confused expression.

Smirking, I ignored her and climbed out of the car, making my way over to her side.

After last night, I wanted to spend some time with Brenna. If we were going to do this, I didn't want any doubt between us. I also needed to see how she did with my son. I know she said she was all in, but I needed to be sure. I couldn't have another person come into his life and mistreat him.

After opening her door, I went to the back and grabbed DJ out of his car seat.

"You mind holding him for a moment?" I asked her, kissing my son on the top of his head.

She glanced down at DJ, and I noticed a small grin on her face. With a slight nod, she held her arms out. I knew she had been around him with my sister, but this was the first time I saw her hold him. I couldn't front that it didn't make my heart expand against my ribcage.

Before shutting the back door, I grabbed his diaper bag and walked to the back of my car. Popping the trunk open, I pulled DJ's stroller out and opened it.

"A'right, you can put him in." Brenna and my son seemed to be having their own private conversation. He was smiling and babbling while grabbing for her face. A genuine smile was on her face while she baby talked and laughed with him.

His babble grew louder when she tickled his stomach.

Outside of my sister and mom, and now Kaia, he never had a female interact with him like this. It caused an unfamiliar wave of emotions to shoot through me.

"DJ, I know you ain't over here tryna take my girl?"

Brenna looked up at me. "Tell your daddy you're just so cute and chunky, you might succeed." She stuck her tongue out and tickled his stomach again.

"Yeah, a'right, hand him here." I chuckled with my arms out.

Brenna handed me my son, who whined and tried to get back to her. "Damn, you really want my girl." I kissed his cheek and put him in the stroller.

"He knows a catch when he sees one." She winked at me.

Lifting one corner of my mouth, I shook my head. "If yo ass says so."

Brenna giggled and laced her arm through mine as we started

for the entrance of the aquarium. I had been wanting to bring DJ here for a while now but didn't have the time. Now that my schedule was more routine, we could do this along with a few more things off the list.

———

"A'right, Ryder, give me one more set than you can break." I let Ryder, a shooting guard for the Titans, know.

I watched as he pushed his legs up on the machine, watching closely in case he struggled.

I was out in *New Haven,* where the wealthy lived. He was doing an in-house session at his home gym in his basement.

My phone vibrated in my sweats, gaining my attention for a moment. When I pulled it out, I saw it was Kaia. She never called when I was working, so I knew it had to be important.

"A'right, you're good. Take a break."

Stepping off to the side, I hit the green button. "Kaia, is everything okay?"

"Your son's mom brought the police here, and they're trying to take DJ!" she rushed out.

My heart dropped to my stomach. "I'll be right there!"

Swiftly turning around, I faced Ryder. "I got a family emergency and gotta go," I spoke quickly. I'm sure he could hear my heart pounding in my chest.

He stopped drinking his water and stared at me. "Yeah, man, go ahead." He nodded.

Like a fire was lit under me, I quickly gathered my things and hurried out of his house. It would take roughly 45 minutes to get back to Butter Ridge Falls, but I was about to make it thirty. Tia had lost her damn mind coming to my house with this bullshit.

———

The moment I pulled into my driveway, I felt my blood grow hotter. Jumping out of the car with balled fists, I stormed over to the circus going on in my yard.

"Tia, what the fuck is this!" I shouted, stepping towards her.

"Sir, step back." The police officer stepped in front of her. She stood behind him with a smirk on her face and arms crossed. "Are you the father?"

My eyes dropped to his waist, where his gun was. Thankfully, he hadn't attempted to reach for it. "Yeah, I am." I gave him a smug look.

"Tae!" I turned as Kaia came rushing out of the house with DJ in her arms. I instantly took him from her and held him protectively.

"There goes my baby! Give him to me!" Tia shouted.

"I ain't giving you shit!" My eyes narrowed.

"Sir, Ms. Gardner called and said you kidnapped her child and-"

"I'm his fucking father! How the fuck can I kidnap him!" My attention snapped to Tia. "What the hell is wrong with you?"

"You're trying to take my son away from me, and I'm not letting you."

"You don't give a fuck about *my son*."

"Sir, Ms. Gardner informed us that you have no rights to the child. Is that correct?" I bit the inside of my jaw.

"We're going to court to change that." A sympathetic look appeared on his face.

"Unfortunately, until the courts decide, legally you cannot withhold your son from his mother. If she wants him back, you have to hand him over." An acidic taste built up in my stomach.

"She's not taking my son."

"If you don't hand the infant over, I'll be forced to arrest you." This time his hands went to his waist.

I gritted my teeth while Tia smiled like she had won.

My eyes dropped to my son, who was oblivious to everything. I looked around my yard again. His partner was standing off to the side, waiting to see how I would react.

My stomach twisted.

"Tae," Kaia spoke lowly behind me.

I wanted to fight this, but I knew it would only make it worse for DJ.

"I'm sorry, son." I kissed the top of his head. "I'll see you soon."

Regretfully, I held my son out for the police officer to take.

He grabbed DJ and passed him to Tia. "Where's his stuff?"

"You ain't taking shit I bought for him."

"You ain't shit!" she yelled, causing DJ to cry.

My heart squeezed, knowing she wasn't going to comfort him properly.

"I'll see you in court," I warned her.

Tia rolled her eyes and turned around, going to a car I wasn't familiar with.

"Tae," Kaia spoke again.

"You can head home," I told her, feeling defeated.

Dropping my head, I turned and walked towards my house. I didn't want to hear shit anyone else had to say. Tia had gone too far. I didn't know if her end game was to hurt me, but she had succeeded. She knew my son was my heart and that taking him from me would hurt me.

My heart was heavy in my chest.

I could only hope my son wouldn't suffer too much in his mother's hands.

eleven

Brenna

"TT, watch what I learned this week!" Bailey shouted, rushing to the grass field.

"I'm watching."

She did a flip, then a back bend, before landing in the splits. "Wow, Bai Bai! Gymnastics is really paying off."

"Hell, it better for as much as we pay," Aisha muttered, making me giggle and glance at her.

She was moving Brooklyn's stroller back and forth.

I met them at the park after being in meetings all day. I had some pretty exciting events coming up that I was thrilled about. One was an engagement party for the rapper Kazier. I had a total fan girl moment when I met him and had to quickly tone it down. He saw what I did for Gage and Aisha and had his team reach out to me.

"Have you spoken to my brother?" Aisha asked me.

A sharp pain shot through my chest as I slowly shook my head.

She sighed. "So, he's blocking everyone out."

My head tilted. "You haven't spoken to him either?"

She shook her head. "No. Me, my parents, and Gage have all

tried calling and getting ahold of him, but all he does is text us that he's good."

Sadly, that's all I've been getting too. When I heard about Tia's antics, I immediately reached out to Tae, but my calls went unanswered. He'd only texted me since the incident too. I tried popping up at his house and knocking, but he ignored that too. I know his son was his world and not knowing if he was being properly taken care of was hurting him, so I was trying not to take his actions personally.

"I swear I hate Tia. If I see her, I'm beating her ass," Aisha spat with her face balled up.

I nodded, agreeing with her.

Tae was an amazing father and didn't deserve this. "I plan on popping up on him today though. He's been blocking us out for days now. I need to make sure he's good."

"I could go," I blurted out. "I just need his key and I'll pop up on him."

She smirked at me. "I'm sure he'd rather have you there comforting him anyways." Aisha grabbed her purse from the bottom of the stroller while I looked around until I saw Bailey was now swinging with some other little girl.

"Here." Aisha handed me the key.

Grabbing it from her, I slid it into my pocket. "He told me he loves me," I confessed lowly.

"My brother?" Aisha's eyes bucked.

Smiling softly, I moved my head up and down.

"I was in shock too when he said it, but I felt it deep down in my soul."

I've had guys tell me they love me before, but something felt different when Tae told me. It was like our souls connected and he took possession of a piece of me that I didn't want back.

"Damn, so when y'all deflowered my house, it was serious, huh?" She bunched her nose up.

I laughed at her choice of words.

"Would you please stop bringing that up!"

She giggled and looked towards the park to locate Bailey.

"I'm happy that the two of you are making each other happy." My chest grew warm.

My best friend's approval of my relationship with her brother was important to me. I would never allow a guy to come between us. Knowing she accepted us and was rooting for us had me cheesing until my cheeks hurt.

———

I stepped inside Tae's dark house and was greeted by silence. The air was stale and gloomy.

Closing the door behind me, I kicked my sandals off and walked through the foyer, making my way to the kitchen to set the food I'd brought over on the counter. I wasn't sure if he had been eating and wanted to make sure he was good for a few days.

Slowly I trekked my way to Tae's room. The door was closed, but I could hear murmurs on the other side.

Pushing the door open, I saw Tae sitting up in his bed. The glow from the TV on the wall illuminated him.

His eyes left the TV for a moment and landed on me. I expected some kind of reaction from him, but his face remained vacant.

I pushed the feelings of rejection from my mind and walked into the room towards his bed. My heart broke seeing the empty look in his eyes.

"Hey," I spoke lowly.

Silence.

Swallowing hard, I climbed on his bed and straddled his lap. Grabbing his face, I forced him to look at me.

"I'm here for you," I let him know.

His eyes peered through me. He barely blinked.

Leaning in, I wrapped my arms around him and hugged him. He didn't reciprocate my hug immediately, but I didn't care. Just being this close to him and feeling his heartbeat against my chest was enough for me.

I closed my eyes and inhaled a deep breath.

Tae smelled like his body wash which was good. At least he was still taking care of himself.

My thumb brushed against the nape of his neck, and I pressed my lips against the top of his head.

It took a while, but Tae finally wrapped his arms around my waist and hugged me tightly.

"I miss my son," he spoke lowly in a raspy, defeated voice.

My heart broke even more.

Pulling back, I grabbed his face again. His eyes were sad. The glow they used to have was nonexistent. I pressed my lips against his, kissing him hard.

"I'm here for you, and it's going to be ok. You're going to get him back." He sighed against my lips and placed his forehead against mine.

I didn't like seeing Devontae like this. He was always a take charge kind of man, but he looked defeated and out of it right now.

"Thank you for coming."

I smiled. "Of course."

I ended up staying the night at Tae's house. I was glad I packed a bag beforehand. We sat around in his room watching the sports channel and eating the Chicken Alfredo I brought over. He was still in low spirits, but it seemed having me there gave him a little peace.

My hand was in his, and every so often, he brought it to his lips and kissed it. My heart fluttered each time.

Tae was strong, so I knew he would get through this, just like I knew DJ would be back in his care where he belonged.

———

"Cousin!" Nova Rae stood up as I approached the table she was sitting at.

"Hey!" The two of us hugged before taking a seat. "You are glowing!"

A bashful smile formed on her face as she waved me off.

"I ordered you a mango passion green tea since I know coffee isn't your thing." I glanced at the clear cup on the round table.

"Thank you."

I sat my bag down and started pulling things out. Nova Rae sat across from me sipping her coffee.

"I don't remember the last time I was in here." Lifting my head, I observed *Java Books*, inhaling the strong coffee scent.

"I love this place. I don't know what I would do without it." Snickering, I pulled out my iPad and flipped the case.

"Okay, so here's what I was thinking based on what you told me."

Today I was meeting with Nova to go over the details of her bridal party. She was engaged to her fiancé Grayson. Even though I wanted to stay in bed with Tae all day, I knew I couldn't cancel on Nova Rae. For one, she was my cousin. Secondly, it was unprofessional. Thirdly, I knew how important this all was for her. Grayson was her soul mate. The two were tying the night next month in September. Her bridal party was in two weeks.

Pulling up the mockup app, I scrolled until I got to her name and handed it over to her.

Eagerly Nova grabbed the iPad and began looking over my ideas. She wanted her wedding to be neutral colors. Browns, tans, and soft pinks, so that's the theme I followed for her bridal shower as well.

While she looked over my iPad, I glanced at my phone. I knew Tae wouldn't have texted me because he was asleep when I left his house. After spending all day in bed yesterday, I dreadfully pulled myself out of it this morning to meet my cousin. He was still in a somber mood, but I got him to at least reach out to his family and ease their mind.

Tae didn't talk much while I was at his house. He seemed to be lost in his head most of the time, but I didn't mind.

"Brenna, this is so cute!" She gushed with glossy eyes.

"Are you about to cry?"

She wiped her eyes and blushed. "No, I'm just excited! I'm getting married to my best friend, my other half, the only guy who has ever made me feel loved and secure. It's all finally starting to sink in."

A wide grin formed on my face. I couldn't be happier for my cousin. Not only was she about to marry the love of her life, but she was also a successful clothes designer and boutique owner.

"I have to go to New York next week to meet with Genesis's team to discuss my fall collection, but I would like to meet up one more time before the shower, if that's fine."

I nodded. "Look at you becoming a big shot designer! I'm so proud of you, boo!"

"Stop!" She lowered her head bashfully and then handed me my tablet.

"I'm wearing something from your line right now." The sundress I had on was from her boutique but also from The Nova Rae Collection.

"You've always supported me. I really do appreciate it, Brenna."

I waved her off. "Girl, you know it's nothing."

We hung around *Java Books* going over a couple more things and catching up on life before I left to head back to Tae's and Nova back to her boutique.

So many people were in love and starting their lives and families. I couldn't wait until it was my turn.

————

"B, I ain't really tryna be out and about right now," Tae complained as I pulled him towards the *Botanical Gardens* entrance.

"I've been wanting to come here for a while, and you needed to get out of the house, so it's a win-win for both of us." When we arrived at the ticket booth, I went into my crossbody purse to grab my wallet, but Tae was already handing the guy behind the glass his card.

"I was supposed to pay." I mugged him.

His shoulders lifted as he grabbed the card along with our tickets.

"When you're with me, you ain't paying for shit."

Rolling my eyes, I grabbed his hand and pulled him through the grassy archway.

"Let's start with the Sun Garden." I pointed to the right of us.

Tae didn't look too happy, but he didn't protest either.

————

"Be honest; today was nice, right?" I questioned before taking a bite of the chicken sandwich.

We explored most of the gardens, all of which were breathtaking. Each one we went to was different from the previous one. The flowers and sculpted plants were beautiful.

Now we were in the café inside the building. After this, I planned on us ending the day with miniature golf.

Tae looked up at me and leaned back in his chair. He didn't speak right away and an unreadable expression was on his face.

My stomach flipped, thinking maybe he wasn't enjoying himself. From what I'd seen, he was having a good time. I had forced him to take a bunch of pictures with me and even got him to smile in a few of them.

"I appreciate you doing this today," he finally responded, easing my nerves.

"Really?" I tilted my head slightly.

His head bobbed.

"I've been driving myself crazy thinking what my son could be going through, and being stuck in the house wasn't helping. I needed to get out and get my mind off everything, if even for a second." Tae leaned forward and reached over, placing his large hand on top of mine.

"I know you're busy with work and have a lot going on, but you putting me first and being here for me means a lot to me."

I was overcome with emotion.

"I told you I was here for you. You're always there for everyone when they need you. This time you deserved that same courtesy. When I love someone, it's real and it's strong. I don't take that word lightly. I don't like seeing you upset, Tae, and anything I can do to help lift your mood, I will."

He didn't reply right away.

Flipping my hand over, I grabbed his. "You're going to get DJ back and everything will be fine. I know it's hard not to, but don't worry, it'll all work out."

His jaw slightly tightened. "I just hope he's cool."

My chest tightened. "I believe he is. We just have to think positive."

"I love you. You know that, right?"

A smile found its way onto my face and I nodded. "As long as you know."

The butterflies in my stomach intensified. The way Tae was staring at me had me in a chokehold. It was intense but full of passion and love. I could feel my heart pounding in my ears.

I cleared my throat, feeling a rush of emotions shooting through me. "Hurry up and eat so I can kick your ass in mini golf."

A slight grin formed on his face. "Yeah, a'right." He removed his hand from mine.

Although it wasn't a full smile, I was happy to see something other than the blank expression that's been on his face these past few days. I was prepared to do whatever I had to do to keep him in high spirits.

twelve

Devontae

"BAI BAI, you can only get two things. Your mom isn't about to yell at me again," I explained to my niece as we stepped into *ChocoLUXE*.

"Okay!" She called out, already rushing into the door.

Shaking my head, I headed for the counter to wait for her. Even though I told her she couldn't go overboard, I knew she was going to grab more than two things.

Today was only the second time I left the house since Tia came and snatched my son away from me. I had attempted to call her a few times without getting any response.

My lawyer had told me to keep a calm head, but it was hard. It's been seven days without my son and it was driving me crazy. I wouldn't be worried if Tia were a responsible mom, but I knew she wasn't. I know she didn't properly take care of my son as she should, and every time I think about what he could be going through, I have the strong urge to wring her damn neck.

Aisha had texted me asking if I could take Bailey to gymnastics and keep her afterward. She was backed up with a big order at her shop, and Gage was at practice.

It was then I realized I hadn't spent any time with my niece in a while, which was unlike me. I had been so caught up in being a dad and my life that I pushed my niece to the side. Once I agreed, I pushed how I was feeling to the side and prepared to spend time with Bailey. I was hoping getting her would help get my mind off DJ being with Tia.

"Tae, hey!" I was knocked out of my thoughts when Ayame's voice sounded behind me.

Without my permission, my eyes scanned her body. She had twins a few months ago and the weight they put on her did her right. She was already slim because of running and working out, but now she was slim thick.

"Wassup Ayame." I tossed her a head nod while focusing on her face.

When I first met Ayame, I was going through my shit with Brenna and wanted to shoot my shot until I found out she was with Austin.

"I hope you have some openings because I'm going to be hitting you up soon," she replied. "I need to tone up some of this baby fat."

I bobbed my head, running my eyes over her frame once again. I personally didn't think anything was wrong with her. The weight looked good on her and she carried it well.

"You have my number. Just hit me up."

She grinned at me. "I will. I miss working out."

Her hand brushed over her short hair. "You letting your hair grow?" Normally she kept it short with tapered sides. Her haircut made me think of Brenna and how fine she looked with her new pixie cut.

"Hell no. I thought I was going to, but it's not for me. Austin's going to cut it for me when I get home later." She pushed a piece of hair out of her eyes.

"Can I get chocolate pretzels too?" Bailey rushed to me.

I raised an eyebrow, seeing she had more than two things in her hands. "Bailey, I said pick two treats."

She gave me an innocent pout. 'But they're small." She showed me the candies in her hand.

Groaning, I shook my head once she batted her eyelashes. Bailey has had me wrapped around her finger since she was born.

"Your mom is gonna beat my ass," I muttered, turning to Ayame.

She had an amused look on her face. "Hey Bailey!"

"Hi!" Bailey waved, setting her things on the counter.

Without me having to tell her, Ayame was already heading for the pretzels behind the display case.

"Y'all have any chocolate grapes?" I asked, grabbing my wallet.

"I think I have two half dozens left."

"Let me get them too.

My hand went over my head. It reminded me that I needed to make an appointment at the barbershop.

"We're going to go get something to eat before you eat all this, okay?" I looked down at Bailey.

She had already opened one of the suckers but nodded her head at me.

Chuckling, I shook my head.

Ayame finished getting our things and rung us up.

I loved spending time with Bailey. Before Gage came into the picture, she was my road dog. Whenever I had free time, I made sure to get her. I never wanted her to feel like she was missing out because she didn't have a dad. Aisha was my heart, and when she had a daughter, that love instantly migrated to her.

Bailey hugged my leg. "I love you, Uncle Tae!" She grinned up at me.

My hand went over the braids in her head. "I love you too, Bai Bai."

Yawning, I pulled into my garage and turned my car off. I had OD'd in the gym today after having three clients earlier. My body was sore and my eyes heavy. The only thing that helped keep my mind off my son was working out.

I grabbed my phone off the passenger seat and saw Brenna had texted me. She was finishing up an event and then heading to my house.

Another yawn left my mouth as I made my way to the door that led into my house. The only thing I wanted tonight was a shower and to be buried deep in my girl.

I kicked my gym shoes off and walked across my house towards my bedroom when a noise stopped me. My brows dipped together when I thought I heard soft cries.

"I'm trippin'," I mumbled, looking around.

The cries seemed to be coming from near the front door.

Making a U-turn, I headed for the front door. The closer I got, the clearer the noise became.

My heart pounded loudly and sweat formed on my forehead.

Quickly I snatched my door front open. My eyes widened and my heart dropped when I laid eyes on my son. He was in a car seat that he clearly had outgrown. His face was bright red as he cried loudly.

"What the fuck!" I hurriedly unhooked him. I picked up the note that was on top of him and lifted him.

"Shit!" I held him up and examined him.

He smelled horrible. He had on a onesie, and I could tell by the soiled diaper it had been a while since he'd been changed.

I bit down on my back teeth as tears filled my eyes. "Daddy's got you, big man. It's okay," I said lowly, attempting to keep my anger at bay.

My blood was boiling as fury filled me.

As if my voice was a switch, DJ's eyes snapped open and small whimpers left his mouth.

"I got you." I kissed the top of his head.

Swiftly kicking my door closed, I turned and rushed upstairs so I could clean him up.

I wasn't sure what the fuck Tia was thinking just leaving my son on my porch. I didn't know how long he was out there, but all I saw was red when I thought about what could have happened to him. My jaw ached from the constant clenching.

"Baby!" I heard from downstairs as I rinsed DJ off. She had gotten my key from my sister and kept it, which I didn't mind.

"Upstairs!" I called out.

Under his neck was filthy as if he hadn't been bathed in days. The onesie he had on barely fit, and his diaper was on its last leg. I had made sure to snap pictures of his state before putting him in the bath.

Once I stripped him out everything and got him in the water, he seemed to calm down. His cheeks were still flushed and eyes puffy, but he was now happily playing in the water.

My heart tugged as I stared at my son. It had only been a week but I could only imagine what he went through during that time.

"Hey, I-DJ? But how?"

"I'll explain later." I kept my eyes on my son. "You mind making him a bottle?" This time I glanced over my shoulder at her.

Her mouth parted but she nodded and walked out of the bathroom.

"A'right, big man, let's get you dressed."

All the crying must have tired him out. Even though he hungrily ate his bottle, which had me wondering whether he ate with his mom, he was asleep within minutes.

I softly stroked his head, afraid to walk away from him. I hated he had to go through this. Although he was young and wouldn't remember, it still pained me.

"He's not going anywhere. Let him sleep," Brenna spoke softly from the door.

My shoulders fell as I pushed out a deep breath. I knew she was right.

Bending down, I kissed the top of his head, then pulled back, staring at him a little longer. I made sure the baby monitor was on before exiting his bedroom.

Brenna looped her arm through mine as soon as I was in the hallway, but I wanted more. Turning around, I pulled her into my chest and hugged her tightly.

My body was tense.

My mind was swirling and my nerves were racing.

"Let's take a shower." She rubbed my back.

I swallowed hard and nodded.

My emotions were all over the place right now. I was angry, happy, and sad all in one. My son was now with me and safe, but that didn't take away how I found him. Tia's ass better stay away from us if she knew what was good for her. I didn't hit women, but my hand itched to slap the fuck out of her. If I had anything to do with it, she would never lay eyes on my son again.

I called my lawyer and left a message for her to call me. Tia's ass was finished, and I would make sure of it.

———

All he does is cry and I can't take it anymore. I'm moving to LA to pursue my career as an actress. He's your problem now.

I kept rereading the note Tia left on top of my son. She left him on my porch for God knows how long to run off and be an *actress*.

My fist balled up, crumpling the paper in the process.

"Baby," Brenna softly called out to me.

I felt her behind me and soon her hands were on my shoulders.

"Fuck her. This is all the proof you need to make sure she

can never take your son again." My head dropped as I enjoyed the way her small, delicate hands felt on my bare skin.

She bent down and placed a kiss on the side of my face.

"I hate that bitch and regret ever sticking my dick in her."

Again, Brenna kissed the side of my face. "No, you don't because you wouldn't have your son."

Reaching behind me, I grabbed her arm and pulled her in front of me. She settled on my lap, facing me. Her arms went around my neck.

Nuzzling my face into her neck, I inhaled her fresh scent. We had just gotten out of the shower, and I loved the fruity body wash she used.

"He's the only good thing that came from her." I pressed my lips against her skin and lifted my head.

"Thank you. Not just for today but all week." Brenna had been to my house every day making sure I was good. Waking up and falling to sleep with her didn't take away the stress of my son not being here, but it brought me comfort.

"Of course." A small toothless grin formed on her face. "I love you."

My eyes searched her.

I knew her words were true. The shining softness in her eyes as she gazed at me showed me so. Not only that but her actions.

One of my hands went to the back of her neck, and I pulled her into me, kissing her hard.

"I love you too."

My son was home and I had my girl. Those were the only two things that mattered to me at the moment. Once I talked to Diya and got everything sorted with me gaining full custody, I was going to work on making things with Brenna more permanent. I didn't want to waste time with her anymore. I knew she was who I wanted, and I was ready to take the next step to secure her position in my life.

thirteen

Brenna

"IT'S OFFICIAL, Mr. King, you have full custody of your son." Diya smiled, staring at Tae.

I reached over and grabbed his hand, giving it a light squeeze. "So, it's over? Tia can't come and take my son from me again?"

The desperation in his eyes pierced my heart.

It's been two weeks since Tia dropped DJ off on his porch, and every day since then Tae has been on edge. He's hardly let DJ out of his sight. There were days he would cancel and reschedule clients so he wouldn't have to leave. It pained me to see him like this. Tae was a strong man, he had a huge heart, and loved his family more than himself. I knew there wasn't anything he wouldn't do for them. Having his son taken away from him and him being mistreated took a toll on him.

Tae's eyes cast over to me briefly. His thumb stroked the top of my hand while I gave him a reassuring smile.

"She has no rights to your son. Not only did the note prove she gave up custodial rights, but she also has a warrant out for child neglect, abandonment, and endangering the welfare of a child. It's over."

Tae's shoulders fell forward. I could see the weight he's been under being lifted.

"Thank you," he pushed out in a strained, gruff voice.

Diya shook her head. "You're a great father, Tae. I decided to pursue family law because I've seen too many great fathers be screwed over by the system. Unfortunately, the system is made to favor mothers. When I see a father who has stepped up and wants to be a father, I make it my goal to assist them however I can. Your son is lucky to have you. Few men go the legal route. They allow their child's mother to drive them away, and they cut themselves out of their kid's life instead. All that worrying isn't necessary anymore. Your son is with you for good."

I watched Tae's Adam's apple rise then fall as he clenched his free hand. His nose expanded and his eyes closed.

"It's over," he whispered, staring at me with hopeful eyes.

With a small smile on my face, I reassured him, "It's over, baby."

———

"My grandbaby is the cutest thing," Candace gushed as we stood on the sidelines of the photoshoot she set up.

"My son looks just like me. What do you expect?" Tae bragged with a cocky grin on his face.

Rolling my eyes, I shook my head and looked back at the kids.

Bailey was holding her sister, and DJ was sitting up next to them, babbling away.

"A'right now, let's get some solo shots of just the girls, then we'll do DJ." Grayson lowered the camera from his face and glanced over at us.

Aisha and Tae walked over to their kids while I stood near Candace. Gage had practice and wasn't able to make it.

"So, you and my son, huh?" Candance asked after a few seconds.

I glanced at the woman I considered a second mom and bashfully nodded my head.

A smirk formed on my face. "Mhm, and it's serious?"

Again, I nodded while tugging on my bottom lip with my teeth. It was surreal that I was having this conversation with her right now. I've known her for the majority of my life. When I was younger, I always thought Tae was attractive, but I never looked at him like I do now. Of course, I was around him since Aisha and I were so close. I saw his mannerisms, how he would date a bunch of different women, and how he walked with confidence no matter what he was doing. I also saw the guy who would go to hell and back for his family, especially his sister.

Although he used to run through women like water, he was never disrespectful to them.

A small snicker left her mouth. "Who would have thought my kids would fall for their sibling's best friend?" She shook her head. "You love him?"

My heart expanded in my chest. My eyes shifted to where he was standing off to the side with DJ in his arms as Aisha worked with her kids to get them in position. He was smiling brightly while bouncing his son.

It was hard to believe that I didn't want anything to do with him a few months ago because he was about to become a father. I thought that him having a kid would change things between us. It was hard to imagine sharing him with not only a kid but another woman also. Those thoughts haunted me for a while.

Still, I had to realize I was more miserable without him. Randy was a good distraction at the time, but there was never any passion or sparks between us. The moment I finally stopped being stubborn and let Tae back in, the light that had been missing reappeared in my life.

"I do," I finally responded.

"And my grandson?" She asked with concern etched on her face. "It's not easy being with a man who has a child. Are you ready for that? I've known you damn near your whole life, Brenna, and I've always looked at you as my daughter. I know my son is in good hands with you, but are you willing to step up with his child?"

I didn't answer her right away. Again, my eyes shifted to the photo shoot.

This time DJ was in front of the camera. They had placed a few blocks down for him to interact with.

"I am," I responded with confidence.

These past couple of weeks of spending time with both Tae and DJ had been fulfilling. I was afraid that Tae wouldn't have time for me anymore and that I would get pushed to the side once he became a dad, but it was anything but that. Although he couldn't drop everything and the two of us couldn't go out on a whim anymore, he always made time for me. If I'm being honest, Tae spoiled me with attention. I never felt as if I wasn't a priority to him.

"I hope so. That Tia girl-" Candance paused and pushed a heavy breath out. "She did a number on my baby and my grand-child. I'm not saying you have to step up and be his mother, but the more you're around, the more I'm sure it'll naturally happen. Tae's a family man. Even though I know he played the field, I know my son is meant to have a family of his own. He's his father's child. I don't want anyone else to hurt either of them."

"They're safe with me, Ms. Candance. I was unsure at first, but now I'm positive this is where I want to be. I've known Tae my whole life. I know what he has to offer. That's what I want."

The corners of her mouth finally rose again and she nodded. "You're a catch, Brenna. My son is lucky to have you." She walked off and headed over to where her kids and grandkids were. Grayson had also walked over to them, showing them his camera screen.

Candance might think Tae was the lucky one, but I wasn't so sure. He opened my mind to something I wasn't sure I wanted and showed me how beautiful it could be. Even though being a mother was far down on my list, and I wasn't even sure if I wanted my own kids, I knew I would always have him and DJ.

———

"I don't understand why we're here," I questioned Tae as my eyes traveled around the room.

His sister was keeping DJ for the weekend, and he told me to pack a bag and meet him in the car. He drove about four hours away to *Sweet Haven* and pulled up to a woody area. I was skeptical when he turned down a road surrounded by trees with barely any lighting, until a compound of cabins came into view.

He pulled up to the biggest one and had me wait in the car. A few minutes later, he was back in the car. When we pulled up to one of the cabins and he cut the car off, I was blown away.

Tae slowly made his way toward me. Each step he took caused my heart to pound louder and my pulse to race.

"Because I know I haven't been the easiest nigga to deal with this past month. The shit with Tia had my mind fucked up, and I was on edge and distant, but you stayed by my side though. I know you were skeptical of this at first, but you didn't run away, and for that, I'm grateful. I just wanted a weekend with just me and you. Somewhere where we can leave the bullshit back home, and we can just enjoy each other's company." His hands gripped my hips securely and he gave me a small tug, pulling me closer to him.

Air fled my lungs.

A need for him roared inside me. Heat rushed up my body finding its way to my cheeks.

"I love you, Devontae King." I made sure to keep my eyes locked on his.

He licked his lips and gave me a crooked grin. "I love you too." He quickly pecked my lips and stepped back.

"I have something for you." He dug into his pocket and pulled out a box.

My eyes widened. "Tae," I whispered breathlessly.

My heartbeat rang in my ears as my throat grew tight.

"It's not an engagement ring. At least not yet."

Not yet.

A shiver shot down my spine.

Tae opened the box and revealed a key.

Confusion filled my face.

"I know you still have my sister's key or whatever, but I wanted to give you something more permanent from me." His Adam's apple moved up and down.

"I want you to move in with me and DJ." I inhaled a deep breath. "I want to build with you, wake up and go to sleep with you every night and morning. I want you in my space all the time, whenever either of us aren't working. I already saw what it was like without you, and that's something I don't want to experience again." He paused and pulled on his bottom lip.

"I don't want to force you into being a stepmom or anything, and I know what I'm asking is a big step, but I've seen you with my son. He loves you and is always happy when you're around. Move in with us and make the two of us complete."

I was sure my heart was about to jump out of my chest. Adrenaline rushed through my veins and my blood thrummed faster.

"Tae."

He stepped closer to me. "Move in with me."

My words escaped me.

My eyes threatened to water, but I forced it back.

Since my words seemed to fail me, I nodded my head.

"Yes?" he asked.

"Yes, I'll move in with you and DJ." I threw my arms around him and kissed him passionately.

He dropped the box and hugged me tightly.

"Fuck me, Tae," I begged as heat rushed to my center. Desire built between my legs.

"Nah, I don't want to fuck you."

I was about to protest until he backed us up until my knees bumped into the bed. "I wanna make love to you."

That night Tae did exactly what he said. He fucked me slowly, and each time he pushed into me or connected his lips with mine, I knew how much he loved me. My body submitted to him, melting against him as if it wanted to cover him. Tae cherished my body in ways I had never experienced before, bringing tears to my eyes.

Something shifted between us that night. If I had any doubts about us, they were easily erased.

Tae had shown me that my heart was safe with him, and I was ready to accept all the love he had to give.

epilogue

Epilogue

Epilogue

DEVONTAE STEPPED into his house expecting to see his son and Kaia but was greeted by silence, which caused his bushy brows to bunch together.

"Kaia!" He called out, kicking his shoes off and making his way through his foyer. Still surrounded by silence, he made his way upstairs, figuring they might be in his son's room.

He paused when he walked past his bedroom, hearing small whimpers from the other side of my door.

His mouth turned upside down. Out of all the rooms in his house, Kaia knew his bedroom was off limits.

"Kaia, you know you're not supposed to-" His words paused when he noticed Brenna and DJ curled up together in the middle of his bed, asleep.

He blinked a few times at the view in front of him. As far as he knew, Brenna was supposed to be working all day. It had been a little over a month since she agreed to move in with him. Things between the two had been going well. The adjustment didn't take long.

She was great with DJ, and he wasn't shocked. He had seen

her with his sister's kids plenty of times and knew she wouldn't have issues with his son. The two of them had bonded over the month she had been here, bringing him joy. You would never suspect there was hesitation on her part in the beginning.

Taking his phone out, he opened his camera app and took a few pictures. Tae had always been a family man, and coming home to this had his emotions running haywire.

Slipping his phone into his pocket, Tae made his way to the bed.

"B," he leaned down, whispering before peppering kisses on her face down to her neck.

Brenna groaned and shifted.

Her eyes soon fluttered open.

"Hey!" She smiled softly, covering her mouth as she yawned.

"Where's Kaia? I thought you were working all day."

Brenna had kept an eye on DJ multiple times, but most of the time, Tae utilized the babysitter or his parents when they started feeling some type of way. He didn't want to overload her so quickly and make her think he was forcing her into a role.

"I did, but most of it I could do from home. I met with my clients and then came back here." Again, she yawned. Her eyes shifted down to DJ, who was cuddled up against her chest. "I told Kaia she could go, and we came in here so I could get some work done, but I guess that didn't work out too well," she tittered.

It was then Tae noticed the open laptop next to them.

He smiled and leaned down, pecking her lips. "Let me go put him in his crib. I gotta holla at you about something."

"Everything okay?" Brenna's eyebrows bunched together.

He nodded. "Yeah. I'll be right back."

Tae reached over her and picked his son up, who fussed for a moment before resting his head on his dad's chest. Tae kissed the top of his head.

Each time he held DJ, he felt blessed. Tia popping up with the cops and taking his son still haunted him at times, but it was then he remembered that he was DJ's legal guardian and no one could take him away again.

Since then, things have been well. DJ was just as happy as he's always been. Devontae was appreciative that the time with his mom hadn't affected that.

Once DJ was securely in his crib, Tae returned to his room only to find Brenna now in the kitchen.

"I'm heating up some baked spaghetti from last night. You want some?"

Instead of responding, he walked up to her, wrapping his arms around her and pulling her into him.

"I love coming home to you and my son."

"Why do you smell good?" She questioned, causing him to laugh.

"What?"

"I thought you were working. You don't smell like the gym."

Brenna glanced over her shoulder at him with a straight face. Tae's smile grew.

He pressed his lips against hers and tugged on her bottom one with his teeth. "I took a shower at the gym, crazy ass." He kissed her again.

"That better be why." A smile hinted on her face.

"You know better than to even think some shit like that."

Brenna set the container she was holding down on the counter and then turned around. Her arms circled Tae's waist and she craned her neck to look at him.

"I love being here with you and DJ. It feels good not coming home to an empty house."

"I like when you call this home." Tae leaned his head down.

"That's what it is, right?"

He snorted. "That it is, baby." He pecked her lips again.

This time Brenna deepened the kiss by pressing her lips harder against his.

"You said you wanted to talk to me." She pulled back.

Using her thumb, she brushed her lip gloss off his lips.

Tae's arms that were wrapped around her waist tightened. "My lawyer called. Tia was finally caught and is currently locked up."

Brenna's eyes shot open. "What? How?"

He shrugged. "She was pulled over with a busted headlight, and when they ran her name, they saw the warrants. Her ass has been in the city this whole time, and I never knew." Tae shook his head.

Just the thought of the woman who birthed his son put a bad taste in his mouth.

"Hey." Brenna grabbed the bottom of his face. "Fuck her. Karma caught up with her, and now it's time for the law to handle her. DJ's here with us and we love him. He's well taken care of, and that's all that matters. Don't allow yourself to get upset."

Tae stared at Brenna in amazement. A sense of peace consumed him. The way he was gazing at her sent a thrill through her veins and caused her heart rate to skyrocket.

"You're right." He sighed, dropping his shoulders forward. "You've treated him better in the month you've been here than his own mother. I don't know how I'll ever repay you."

Brenna shook her head. "There's no need to thank me. When I agreed to move in, I agreed to be there for you *and* DJ. I meant it when I said I loved him. I enjoy being here with both of y'all and seeing him grow every day. Tia's missing out, but her loss is my gain."

Air fled Tae's lungs. He was tempted to drop down to one knee.

"Fuck I love you, man," he groaned.

Brenna smiled, feeling her heart kick into overdrive.

"I love you too."

The two of them shared a kiss.

They had come a long way, and although the path wasn't clear at first, they were able to find their way back to each other, and now they couldn't picture life without the other.

The end!